AMERICAN VISA

THE THRILLING ESCAPADE

OF

LOVETT AND THE GANG

Amaefuna C. Udechukwu

DEDICATION

THE GREAT WOMEN IN MY LIFE:

Mrs. Elfreda Chizube Okoye - Adannem. My Mother General.
Mrs. Chinweokwu Maledo - Nnem. She turned my life around.
Mrs. Mary Udechukwu - My Daddy's wife.
Mrs. Ifeoma Udechukwu - God anointed my head with oil; my cup over flows.
Pharmacist Hope Chinyelu Nnoli - My one and only special Octogenarian aunty.
Mrs. Theresa Nwakego Shaibu - (Nee Ayomoh), my maternal aunty.
Mrs. Priscilla Chizube Udechukwu - (Nee Nsofor). My grandmother. Ncheta ana echeta onye ezi omume, bu ngozi.
Mrs. Welonwo Ubimago Ayomoh - My maternal grandmother.
Mrs. Patricia Ndidiamaka Udechukwu - (Nee Ayomoh). Odi uko n' mba. My sweet mother. Nnem ezigbo nne.

AND MY ROLE MODELS AND MENTORS.

Dr. Chikwendu Iwe (1960 – 2006) - MD, Founder, RacChigel Veterinary Practice, Aba.
Chief Sir. U. Nnoruka Udechukwu (SAN, KSC) - Ugo. The god who visited us, in the likeness of men.
Pharmacist Ebenezer C. Udechukwu - (1930 – 2015). 'My beloved father, in whom I am well pleased.'
Pa. Amamefuna Samuel Udechukwu - My grandfather. Ife ncheta ebighi ebi, ka onye ezi omume ga abu.

UDECHUKWU n'ede n'mba nine. - (God's fame resounds all over the world).

Your loving spirits sustain me still.

CONTENTS

Dedication
Acknowledgements · i
Foreword · v
Prologue · vi

1 Chapter One: **THE BEGINNING** · 1

2 Chapter Two: **ENTER THE TIGER** · 25

3 Chapter Three: **THE MASTER PLAN** · 32

4 Chapter Four: **FURTHER CONSULTATIONS** · 38

5 Chapter Five: **IMPLEMENTATION** · 48

6 Chapter Six: **ARRIVAL @ MMIA** · 61

7 Chapter Seven: **THE LONE LONG VACATION** · 71

8 Chapter Eight: **THINGS FALL APPART** · 79

9 Chapter Nine: **UWA MGBEDE** · 85

10 Chapter Ten: **REVELATION** · 102

GLOSSARY · 111

QUESTIONS · 112

JOB OF MANY COLORS · 114

ACKNOWLEDGMENTS

For giving me the intellect to dine with authors, kings and queens, to God be the glory. Amen.

My great dad, Pharmacist Ebenezer C. Udechukwu, my sweet mother, Mrs Patricia Ndidi Udechukwu, my wise and wonderful siblings, Chizube, Emeka, Chinweokwu, Uchechukwu, Igwebike and Chinenye. My jolly good cousins, Barrister Chika Nnoli, Dr. Ifeanyi Ayomoh (Jimfranca junior), Chumy Egbuna (my Chairman). Nnukwu nnam ochie, Chief (Honorable) H.C. Nsofor. Your Highness, Engr. H.C. Udechukwu (Obidialo). Chief Patrick Mbanefo Ayomoh (Aganike Showers). My in - laws, Engr. Amechi & Ngozi Ekechuku, (Meche Sings). You gave me the greatest gifts of time and agape love. I appreciate.

I am naturally shy. My friends, just like states, are few in number. They chose me. I remain loyal to you all. Mrs Nancy Nnona, Dr. Chima Agoh (Ace Veterinary Practice). Dr. Nnaka Onwutalu. Akirika Ochendo Dr. Charles C. Ibe DVM, FCVSN. Ambassador, Hon. Dr. Kingsley Ebenyi. Mrs Amaka Chima Kanu. Dr. Chris Emetuobi Ugwu. Dr. Obi Okonkwo (Osha). Dr. Izundu Onyeachonam (Nze Ezuo). Dr. (Mrs)Tayo A. S. Aniagboso (Paws and Claws International). Dr. Simeon Ukagba (Surgeon General). Dr. Justin (Saddam). Dr. Mrs. Rose Ejidike (Queen Amina). Dr Paul Obika (Elder statesman). Dr. James Ezi (Jamina). Dr. Echezona Obieke. Hon. Dr. Harry Oranezi (Wisdom Harry O). Dr. Mark Obinwa (Pets Mart). Engr. Uzoma Anyanwu (Super Plus Engineering). Nze Ifeanyi Umennaihe (Magic finger). Azubike Ndukife (Prince).

M/s Nneka Asoegwu. Mrs Amarachi Grace Okorie.

Mrs Joy ThankGod (Hoplite Veterinary Practice). Mrs Christy Anierobi Richards. Lady Eva Obiora. Mrs. Victoria Thomas (Dominion City Foundation Class).

In 2003, I became a member of Club 25 of Nigeria. I immediately assumed office as Secretary of the Tennis Section. After the Aba branch general elections later, I became the secretary of Aba branch. That led to my baptism in Aba branch as 'Secretary Up & Down'. I was elected the National secretary some years later. I humbly appreciate these men for positively imparting my life: Chief Basil Obiagbawasi Ohaka (Nwadurugbo). Chief Dr. Francis Eneh (Iron T). Elder Reginald and Mrs. Umeike (Ogu Power). Dr. and Dr. Mrs. Cajetan Duru (Perpetual Help). Chief Godfrey Chukwunyere (Onwa). His Eminence Ngozi Ukaegbu. Mazi Joe Asianya . Arch. Ezera Kalu. Barrister Ifeanyi Elenwoke (Elenma eje ogu 2). Chief Sunny Ekpechi (Aka ekpuchi onwa). Chief Eddy Obiukwu (Nwata kwochaa aka). Chief Mathew and Mrs. Obieze (Dakosa). Chief Sir Lawrence Ebere (Anyagharaigwe). Chief Chukwudi Agbazie (Chumoc). Gentle man Dr. Ogbonnaya Amah. Honorable Sylvester Okwara (Manager). Sir Nnaemeka Nchusi (Afu nwa echeta nna). Evangelist Mishak Ubaezuonu (Paparipa). Chief Emeka Omii (Echie eziokwu eze). Sir Austin Morah (Onwa n'etili ora). Chiadikobi Eleazu (Tennis Captain Fantastic). Engr, Ray Johnson. (National President). Ezigbo Nwannem Emeka Chukwuanu (Odaa Opuo). Asi na oburo Jehova, gini ka anyi ga eme. If it had not been Jehova who was on our side.

...Psalm 124; 1 and 2.

My writing potentials also became manifest while I was serving my community as secretary of our family meeting, Nzuko Irefi, Oraifite, Aba branch. I sincerely appreciate the entire members, especially our former chairmen,

Mr. Christian Okolo, Ezinna Basil Udechukwu, Nze Ifeanyi Ezepue and Mr. Ndubisi Okeke. And my predecessor, Mazi Chukwuma Ezepue.

My Fellow choristers elected me their secretary in 1995. I humbly pay tribute to our nonagenarian Archdeacon, Dr. Lawrence Utaegbulam and the entire members of St. Paul's Chapel Choir, Umungasi, Aba.

Special tribute to the unique Doctor of Veterinary Medicine Class of 1992. (#HOMECOMING2022) They also call me Secretary since 1991.

 The evil bondage of 'near-success-syndrome' was broken through Christian fasting and prayers. A million thanks to Venerable Amechi Okwuosa. Rev. Dr. Ramsey Marshall (Kingdom of Power Champions). Brother Prince Nwaturuocha, Bro. Benjamin Idahosa and Brother Babalola Sampson. (GODKIA). I am profoundly grateful to the families of my bigger cousins, Mazi John Mbaegbu (Nnadebeaku) and Hon. Nnamdi and Mrs Ngozi Udechukwu (Odera).

Youths worldwide that will read this book must surely join me in praising God, for the special priestly anointing of Pastor David Ogbueli, Pastor Shola Olapade and Pastor Jude Obiekwe of DOMINION CITY; raising leaders that transform society.

Sir Emeka Emereole, Chairman, Online Hackney Practitioners Association of Nigeria. OHPAN leaders with passion. Our welfare, Our Concern. I remain your boy.

My children read my first novel 'Poultry Events; The amazing story of a macho king', and assured me that they will spread the story to their classmates and school teachers. Odera Daniel Thomas. Obi David Obiora. Ikechukwu Okorie. Godslove and Chidiebere Eleazu.

Emmanel Ezike. Ogbonna Martins Ochor. Amauche Meniru. Chisom. Ginika. Prince. Ebube. Akachukwu (Ndubisi). Emelie, Obumneme, Victor Okoye. Udo, Ugo, Ife Ebenezer. Ugwumsinachi Maledo, Uchechukwu, Adimchukwunobi, Somtochukwu, Anulika. Somadina, Ja'Yaike. Kef and KaObi. Aut viam inveniam, aut faciam. (if you cannot find the way, make one). You are the LIGHT.

Within a short period of my migration from the East to the federal capital territory, Abuja, I learnt so much from the voice of the voiceless, ordinary doctor Ahmad Isah. The President and founder, Brekete family and Human Rights Radio and Television, 101.1 FM. Redefining broadcasting.

Finally, I humbly acknowledge all those who are not mentioned, but had worked quietly, actively and prayerfully to make this publication a dream come true. I pray that all of us will catch the vision; To Prepare Humanity, for Eternity with Divinity.

Amaefuna C. Udechukwu

ONODUGO

FOREWORD.

THIS IS A 'PICK AND CAN'T DROP' STORY. THE READER IS HELD SPELL BOUND BY THE AUTHOR THROUGH HIS POWER OF SUSPENSE.

THE READER IS TAKEN ON A TOUR DOWN THE LANE OF 'MEMORIES OF YESTER YEARS', PLAYING BACK TO YOU (THE READER) A VIVID PICTURE OF YOUR PERSONAL EXPERIENCES IN SCHOOL. FULL OF ADMONITION FOR YOUNGSTERS.

MRS. VICTORIA THOMAS.
The Proprietress
Vidan Creche, Nursery and Primary Schools.
Ajah, Lekki, Lagos.

PROLOGUE;

American visa, The Thrilling Escapade of Lovett and the Gang is a true love and life story. It happened at the various scenes described inside the novel as chapters. There are various songs and old country music mixed with the story. The entire adventure was documented for youths in secondary schools and institutions of higher learning.

This novel is also intended to guide children from the age of eleven into their twenties. This is the age bracket when humans of opposite sexes begin to attract each other. The books they read should be supervised by their parents, guardians and teachers.

The character Maduora portrayed in the story is to guide young boys and girls in taking decisions about the kind of company or gang they are growing up with.

It will encourage parents and guardians to always be there for their children. Purchase of materials money can buy by their mothers, and the paying of school fees by their fathers or guardians, is not always enough in this internet age. We need to spend more time to play, read and travel together with the younger generations.

Above all, lead by example. Do not just show how by pointing and mentioning it alone. Please let's live exemplary lives ourselves. That was the main reason why our Lord and Savior Jesus Christ came to earth to show us the way.

Interlude One recollects the early years of Maduora and Egwuatu as Class One students in the same dormitory at Oracity Grammar School, (Oragram).

InterludeTwo tries to blend Maduora's academic life in the institution of higher learning with his relatively naïve social life outside the school.

In the third interlude, Maduora appears to live in harmony with the academic, social and cultural challenges of his youth.

If you are reading this novel because you want to get an American visa or you love escapades, for sure you will enjoy the storyline, enjoy the suspense of adventure and get the ultimate visa. But before you jump into the Tarzan-like jungle with the gang, let's check some verses of the greatest book ever, The Bible. St. Luke's gospel chapter 4; 4 says;

"And Jesus answered him saying, it is written that man shall not live by bread alone but by every Word of God."

Try to link the above statement with this one. God visited Joshua after the death of Moses and told Joshua the same thing. According to Joshua 1: 8;

"This book of the law shall not depart out of your mouth but you shall meditate therein day and night that you may observe to do according to all that is written therein for then you shall make your way prosperous and then you shall have good success."

Good success comes from reading and meditating on the good book. I started practicing this daily reading and meditating in January 2015. Seven months later, my first novel 'POULTRY EVENTS; The Amazing Story of a Macho King' which was written twenty years earlier was completed and made available to the reading public. Just three months later, my second novel 'AMERICAN VISA' was completed as well.

You can make sure you read **American visa, the thrilling escapade of Lovett and the Gang** several times over. You can recapitulate the story to your friends and loved ones. Stock your children's library with novels like this but make sure you read and meditate on the Word of God daily.

As you can see, if we feed ourselves with the Word of God daily, God grants our daily bread. So ea – easy. Or better still, so simple.

In the olden days and in the jungle, boys on hunting spree usually whistle with their lips. In these modern times, only a few people can still whistle with their lips. More people sing these days than whistle. Now let's sing along as we join Lovett, Maduora, Egwuatu and Posha in the escapade.

CHAPTER ONE

Back through the years, I go wondering once again. Back to the seasons of my youth. I recall .., no.., no.., not the box of rags someone gave to the legendary country music icon, Dolly Parton, and how mummy Parton put the rags to use. Fundamentally too, this is not exactly the '*job of many colors*' by one Nigerian music copycat. He sang how his daddy put his dogs or something to use. He started practice as an animal doctor. In his forties, he delved into various businesses. When he realized himself, he sang a jubilating song titled, *JOB OF MANY COLORS, my daddy made for me.* Who said Nigerians doesn't have comedians. Well, we need to know more about Sam Levenson, Dean Martin and Don Adams of the United States of America.

I just hope you don't mind as I go again, back to the season of my youth. I recall sometime around the wonder months (September, October, November and December) of 1986. In the cool hilly grasslands of the premier university town east of the River Niger, three young adventurous friends and undergraduates of the University of Nigeria, Nsukka, set out to make history.

Two out of the three good friends, Egwuatu and Maduora, were ex-students of Oracity Grammar School, Oracity. Both of them met for the first time as Class One students, far back in 1979. The third member of the '*gang*' is Posha. Maduora and Posha met for the first time in Maduora's hostel room, No. 325 Obafemi Awolowo Hostel, University of Nigeria. The trio was fun loving teenagers.

Egwuatu gained admission into UNN to study Philosophy. Maduora gained admission into the same UNN to study Animal Husbandry just a year after Egwuatu's matriculation. In their early teens and at the Oracity Grammar School days, both of them belonged to the same 1984 graduating class. But in the tertiary institution, as you can see, what God had joined together, the Joint Admissions and Matriculation Board (JAMB) has put asunder. So, while Egwuatu was a second-year undergraduate, Maduora became '*ewu matricula.*'

Most first year students in Tertiary institutions of learning in eastern Nigeria are also known as '*ewu matricula.*' This is mainly because of their relative naivety and the tendency to ask too many questions. Being new in an institution of higher learning, one gradually realizes that there are so many more things to learn. In order not to fall into unnecessary punishment or embarrassment, the first-year students (a.k.a, Jambites or Jambitoes) tend to be very inquisitive. When they run into senior students, especially those that got recently promoted from year one to year two, that's when they are treated like goats because the 'ewu matriculas don't know much about their new environment. Most times, they quickly identify the dining halls first, just like goats identifying their grazing lawns, chop the food and leave the rest to God. Egwuatu had every opportunity to treat Maduora like a goat and he did. Maduora, like many other smart and intelligent chaps was less concerned with trivialities. After all, it was not Egwuatu's fault. What really happened was that these were the two fine boys First School Leaving Certificate (FSLC) had joined together from Class One to Class Five but were academically put asunder by JAMB.

PAUSE;

We wanna be starting something, we wanna be starting something.

We wanna be starting something. Too high to get over, Heeya!

Too low to go under, Heeya!

You stuck in the middle, Heeya! The pain is thunder. . .

Cool it down a bit please. This is not the copycats' copy of Michael Jackson's 1984 Thriller, but really, something enthralling wants to start.

Once upon a date, Maduora went to read in the Faculty of Animal Husbandry library. He came across an old edition of the Newsletter of the International Animal Husbandry Students Association (IASA). He glanced through the Newsletter and decided to become a member of IASA. He copied the mailing address of the IASA from the Newsletter and immediately wrote a letter to the Information Officer of IASA through the headquarters in the Netherlands, Europe.

After a couple of weeks, Maduora got a reply from the Information officer of the IASA. Inside the envelope, there was an official letter acknowledging the receipt of his letter in the Netherlands. Secondly, there was a membership Registration Form which Maduora was required to complete and return to the Netherlands. Thirdly, there was a bank note or a financial document indicating the amount of money required for new membership registration.

Maduora was very excited because he got a prompt reply to his letter. Only very few first-year students could imagine the joy that filled his humble heart. He became joyous because that was his first official letter from overseas. Truly speaking, it was a rare achievement for many undergraduates then, especially those who gained admission into the tertiary institution from the kind of community secondary school Maduora and Egwuatu came from. Maduora was not familiar with any foreign currency and also can't easily determine the exchange rate between the Nigerian naira and the diverse European currencies. He started making enquiries to find out the exact amount in naira. It took him some days to find out the amount in naira required for the new IASA membership registration.

But the truth is that he delayed in completing the membership form because he suddenly found out he can't afford it. He also needed to consult his beloved dad at Enugu before he could make such a financial commitment. Maduora was so much dependent on his dad in taking important decisions during his teenage years. The reason is simply because his dad, a senior civil servant in Nigeria, always made himself available to all his children's needs.

After reading and digesting the contents of the letter from the Netherlands, Maduora spent most of the subsequent days contemplating the exchange rate and the procedures involved in becoming a member of IASA. Maduora was also waiting to hear from his dad probably by the weekend. He kept the letter and its entire content to himself without disclosing anything to his classmates and mixed 'breed' roommates.

On his way to the faculty office one Friday afternoon, he glanced at the small wood partitions where mails are kept for staff and students. He noticed there was something in the students' corner of the partition. He paused and then moved closer. Behold, very far from his wildest expectations, there was a '*letter bomb*'.

The letter bomb was addressed to Maduora Eze. The two major contents of the bomb include;

1.   An informal letter from the information officer of IASA, indicating that Maduora's registration form has not been returned.

2.   The Bomb; A completed STUDENTS' HOLIDAY EXCHANGE form of a female member of IASA who has interest in visiting Nigeria.

Time heals all wounds they say. The very painful physical and emotional wounds are inclusive. Yes, they all heal with time. Likewise, physical beauty and joy fades with time. It was the excitement in Maduora's heart and the highly spirited expression on his face when he saw the passport photograph attached to the students' holiday exchange form that made him describe the second letter from the Netherlands as a letter bomb.

Maduora's initial interest in the IASA is to find a platform on which to improve his studies by travelling abroad. He read from the old edition of the IASA newsletter that IASA organizes holiday exchange programs for student members. This was the first time Maduora learnt that such a thing existed. He never knew, - courtesy of attending a community grammar school. Most of the other students he met at UNN appeared to have had prior knowledge of students' holiday exchange programs.

He read the entire contents of the letter and the bomb several times until he found out that he has been bombed but there was no explosion. He was actually dazed by the contents of the letter and the bomb. Juvenile minds, not to worry, you will later grow up. At this point, Maduora was yet to appreciate what Kenny Rogers meant when he sang The Gambler;

"...You never count your money, when you're sitting at the table. There'll be time enough for counting, when the deal is done."

The informal letter from the IASA information officer required Maduora to inform him quickly if he can play host to the female student who partially indicated interest towards visiting Nigeria. The name of the female student is Lovett Choice Jackson.

Further detail from the student's holiday exchange form includes her passport photograph. This clearly indicated that she's an African American. A citizen of Chicago, United States of America. She had just a year prior to graduation as an Animal Doctor. By Nigerian University standards, she was a fifth-year student of the University of Illinois. She was 20 years old. All these details did only one thing to Maduora.

He was distracted from focusing on his own plan to participate in the holiday exchange program. He thought the only way he could travel is to fill his own copy of the holiday exchange form, get the money from his dad and then travel. Young chap wake up. The silent letter bomb blast cleared from his eyes when he handed over the entire contents of the letter to his fellow roommates. He quietly gave the letter to them one after the other to read. He expected pieces of advice from some of them so that he can decide on what next to do. By the time all seven of them had gone through the letter, it was like the rehearsal of the song they sang on their matriculation day. Using the tune of Yvonne Chaka Chaka's late 80's chat buster song, *"Umqumboti"*, hear them;

We ma Dlamini, Umquom'quobothi (2x).
"Jambites are many, waiting for action. Jambites are many, waiting for action."

The names of the six extra Jambites who were always found in Maduora's room are:

i. Posha Okeke; (a.k.a Poshality). He is a first-year medical student.

ii. Ben Dibia; (a.k.a Dr. Ben).

iii. Nwokoba Dike; (a.k.a Hejike).

iv. Okay Nwobodo; (a.k.a Okay High). v. Christopher Obi (a.k.a Hilltops).

vi. Manuel Obinwa (a.k.a Born Again).

Out of the six names listed above, only Christopher Obi and Nwokoba Dike were the official roommates of Maduora Eze. The seven of them always conglomerate together in room 325 Awolowo Hall due to various funny excuses that Jambites always come up with.

Let me start with Posha Okeke. Poshality was officially assigned to Mbanefo Hall. He meandered his way into the famous room 325 when he claimed that Hejike was his school mate at Federal Government College (FGC), Enugu. Maduora and Hilltops who were the official occupants of room 325 could neither investigate Posha's claim nor query Hejike who brought Posha into their room. Like play like play, Posha started claiming that room 325 is his room. But the truth is that, none of Posha's official roommates at Mbanefo Hall was a Jambite.

Despite his beards which grew luxuriantly, he always felt intimidated by his official roommates at Sir Louis Mbanefo Hostel. He ran away several times from his room at Mbanefo Hall. Sometimes, the senior roommates sent him on 'involuntary exile'. He later found a safe haven in room 325 Awolowo Hall.

Posha Okeke hails from Ubasi town in Anambra State. He was a fine-looking young lad and a very good footballer. Posha played in the defense department for The First Year Medical Students Association (FYMSA) football team. He is well built in all manly capacity as an athlete. Anytime he clears the football out of danger for his teammates, all the spectators, especially the girls will respond to the move by shouting, *"Poshality, Poshality, Posha, Posha, Po sha sha."*

While responding to the spectators who also threw their arms into the air, Poshality blows kisses into the air. He gradually returns to his defense department with a beautiful backward swagger.

Poshality means kindheartedness. He thinks

about the convenience and satisfaction of his neighbor before he takes his own share. Posha is not a greedy man. Posha believes in the dignity of labor. Little wonder he became one of the major characters of this book. On graduation after six years in the medical school, Posha was found worthy in character and in learning.

The truth is that Posha's un-ceremonious exile from Mbanefo Hall to room 325 Awolowo Hall made him a star in this story. Posha's presence in room 325 and the subsequent roles he played as a good Jambite, roommate and friend of Hejike and Maduora, put his name as one of the fun loving trium virate that formed the gang.

Perhaps, the most personal feature of Posha, which makes him stand out in every crowd, is his innocent baby face with luxuriantly growing beards. If you know one of Nigeria's most celebrated highlife music icon, Chief Sunday Akanite (a.k.a Oliver de Coque), his luxuriant beards were more famous than his music. He once claimed that the money he spent making his beards look great was enough to buy him a custom-made limousine. Despite being a teenager, Posha could easily be mistaken as a son of Oliver de Coque.

Above all things, Posha feared God. Posha is a practicing Roman Catholic. Maduora testified that every step he took based on Posha's advice was worth it. At various times during their first year in UNN, Maduora and Posha climbed mango trees together. They went to physical education training together.

One early morning, while both of them were jogging from Sir Francis Akanu Ibiam Stadium UNN, towards a cluster of mango trees, Posha taught Maduora a gyration song to sing and follow him;

"Joggle ba, joggle ba, joggle ba, n'egwu agba go. Joggle ba, joggle ba, joggle ba, n'egwu agba go." (Dance, dance, dance, music has come)

Initially, it sounded like one of Gentleman Mike Ejeagha's folk songs;

"Mbe agaba, Ajambene. Mbe agaba, Ajambene."

Maduora did not know Posha was referring to the ripe mangoes he saw on the cluster of mango trees between New Science Lecture Theatre (NSLT) and Carver Building (Department of Chemistry). Posha started the song and jogged towards the mango trees. Maduora followed him, jogging, learning and chorusing the gyration song. At the same time, he was enjoying the morning parade but jogged to the nearest mango tree before Posha. Posha never knew Maduora liked mangoes more than any other fruit. For his likeness for mango fruits, Maduora's mother and elder sister always call him captain mango.

Posha climbed the mango trees one at a time. He pushed down the ripe fruits with accuracy and dexterity. Maduora collected and kept their harvest safe. That particular day, their early morning jogging session ended as a choir practice cum mini mango feast with other roommates of room 325. As the mango feast and singing progressed inside the room, Maduora would intermittently pause to listen to the other voices. Then he will join the singing again after shouting, "*Louder.*"

The singing usually comes to a low tempo after Maduora's gesticulations like a funny old European choir master without a tailcoat. Till date, Maduora has no regret sharing room 325 or any other thing, spiritual or material with Poshality. That means, after nearly thirty years, Maduora is looking forward for another joggle session with Posha.

Ben Dibia meandered his own way into room 325 Awolowo Hall, nearly the same way and almost at the same time with Posha. He was remarkably taller than Posha and Hejike who were his acclaimed schoolmates at FGC Enugu. He wears medicated or reading glasses. He hails from Imo State. I can't recall whether he was allocated to any hostel like all other first year students. He started sharing room 325 with the six others after telling his own funny escape story to Hejike. Again, Maduora and Christopher could neither investigate his funny excuses nor query Hejike.

Dr. Ben was unique because Maduora had doubts whether he was really a first-year student or not. Dr. Ben presents his points very maturely. Of course, most of the discussions they held in the room centered on women. He used to speak confidently and had strong financial support from home. He is a gentleman to the core. He can be mistaken for a gentle giant. Dr. Ben was also a first-year medical student. So, Posha and Dr. Ben settled in room 325 just because they told Hejike funny, unverifiable, Jambitoes cock and bull stories. Maduora never complained about the crowd brought into their room by Hejike. When Maduora sought Dr. Ben's candid opinion concerning the passport photograph on the holiday exchange form. He frankly said, *"The girl must come."*

Nwokoba Dike (a.k.a Hejike), Christopher Obi and Maduora Eze are the three first year students officially assigned to room 325. Hejike hails from Uba town in Anambra State. He gained admission into UNN to study Biochemistry. His initial course of study is Medicine. But what JAMB has put asunder, may God help us to join together. Hejike wanted to study medicine like the majority of the science inclined candidates. But JAMB put Hejike and medicine asunder. After spending his first year at UNN as a Biochemistry student and a member of room 325, Hejike disappeared. He later gained admission to study medicine at the University of Benin, Mid-West Nigeria. *"JAMB kor, biochem ni."* Hejike just told JAMB;

"Ka ima nka, ima nke ozo?"

(If you know this one, do you know that one?)

Hejike was lightly bearded, dark in complexion and a little chubby. He was a gentleman teenager. His contributions in most of the discussions in the room were mature. His mind was always focused on sitting for the next JAMB exam. Maduora never knew that was Hejike's main pre-occupation until he stopped seeing Hejike. When Maduora sought Hejike's candid suggestions with reference to the passport photograph on the holiday exchange form, he said, "*The girl must come.*"

Maduora thinks the reason Hejike also attracted Okay Nwobodo into room 325 was that Okay was a real member of FYMSA, UNN.

Okay High was the one member of room 325 that Maduora was not exactly sure how he meandered his way into the room 325. Okay High was officially assigned to room 307 but not to room 325. Okay's funny blabbing was that his official roommates in room 307 were all his seniors. What makes his story fit into the cock and bull gist of jambitoes is that Okay High smokes cigarettes. Despite his bad habit of regular smoking, he doesn't feel high enough to withstand his official and legitimate roommates in room 307. They also sent him on involuntary exile several times until he found a new haven in room 325.

His points during discussions in the room were street wise. He was always fearless, very logical and constructive. Unlike Maduora, Okay High grew up in the streets of Enugu. He attended a secondary school at Enugu or near Enugu. He was always sober. He respected Maduora's dad when they met.

Among the seven roommates of the famous room 325, Okay High was the only one who was studying medicine with all the confidence and bravado required of a first-year medical student. He came from a relatively low financial background. But he never displayed poverty. He was always grateful to God that his sister was providing for him. He eventually graduated and is now a practicing medical doctor. His reaction to the passport photograph on the holiday exchange form was, the girl must visit Nigeria.

Christopher Obi once asked Maduora what happened. It was when Maduora returned from lectures one afternoon and discovered that a bunch of bananas he kept in his wardrobe to ripe was missing. Maduora was angry. He did not know who to blame for the missing banana. There were at least seven of them who have uninterrupted access into the room. He quickly met a typist, drafted a warning note and pasted it on the hostel notice board. Part of the warning note read like this:

"... A big bunch of bananas was brutally devoured by the beasts of room 325. The devourer(s) are hereby given 12 hours to identify themselves and replace the banana. Failure to do so will leave the Students Union

Government with no option than to declare room 325 a jungle..."

A second copy of the warning note was pasted on the entrance door of room 325. A third copy was pasted on the wardrobe door.

Out of the seven members of room 325, it was only Hilltop that read the notice while it was on the notice board and eventually asked Maduora what really happened. Other members of the room did not ask. The hungry beasts knew who ate the banana. They knew Maduora was a fellow jambito. Jambitoes can only bla blab bla, and like Maduora who had boasted he had a friend in the Students Union Government (SUG), he can't do anything.

Maduora later told Hilltop how he hid the unripe banana inside his wardrobe. But the other unofficial roommates had access to the wardrobe mysteriously. They couldn't wait for the banana to ripe. They devoured it.

It was fun sharing the experience later among all the roommates. Two of the unofficial roommates told Maduora to hide a new bunch of bananas inside his wardrobe again, they will help him catch the real banana beasts. They all laughed and continued their blabbing.

Hilltop is also an Animal Husbandry student of

UNN. Till today, some Nigerians still wonder why somebody should bother to enter a tertiary institution only to study courses like; Animal Husbandry, Veterinary Medicine, Mosquito Diseases, Oke na Ngwele Psychology, Agwo na Mbe anatomy, Nkita and okuko physiology, Uchicha na awo skeleton, etc, etc. A quick glance at the first verse of one of our Anglican Church hymns might give us a better understanding.

HYMNS;

ANCIENT AND MODERN, NO. 442

"All Things Bright and Beautiful, All Creatures Great and Small, All Things Wise and Wonderful, The Lord God Made Them All."

- Cecil Francis Alexander (1818-1895)

Please permit me to recall again. No..., no..., no..., neither from my own youth nor from Dolly Parton's Coat of Many Colors, I recall this time, from the King James Version of the book of all generations, the Bible. Genesis 1; 25.

"And God made the beast of the earth after his kind and cattle after their kind and everything that creeps upon the earth after his kind and

God saw that it was good".

So, a careful browsing of the Bible will further intimate you that our creator performed the art and science of creating animals before creating humans. In the next verse, let's check again. Genesis 1: 26.

"And God said, *let us make man in our image, after our likeness...*"

As far as Maduora and Christopher are concerned, Nigeria's woes will be turned downside up, if Nigerians will follow God's biblical creation pattern. That means, it is better to study animal medicine before you study human medicine. Brethren, can I hear a clap offering for Nigerian doctors . . . louder please . . . yea . . . yea . . . cool it down please.

Christopher Obi hails from a town very close to the university. He goes to his village every weekend except when he has weekend examination in the department. He attended a community secondary school too. He was naïve and always created the impression he felt inferior to other roommates. He smokes cigarettes in secret. He had Maduora as a confidant. He liked Maduora too. His contributions to discussions in the room were severally made to Maduora privately.

After browsing the passport photograph on the holiday exchange form, he supported the motion by saying, *"the girl must come."* He enjoyed his first year in room 325. Hilltop graduated as a veterinary doctor and has a successful private livestock business.

Manuel Obinwa was referred to as born again because he is. Once upon a time, he was seen inside the New Science Lecture Theatre (NSLT) clutching a very big Bible and preaching the gospel. One evening, he appeared in room 325.

Obinwa and Maduora met at Federal School of Arts and Science (FESAS), Ogoja, Cross River State. They became very close friends. Right from their days at Male Hall One, FESAS, Maduora admired the physical and social qualities of Obinwa. Obinwa stayed in room seven while Maduora was in room one. Obinwa was an athlete and also played football for the FESAS football team. It was Obinwa who came closer to Maduora and they became very close friends. They shared family backgrounds and intimacies while focusing on passing JAMB.

Obinwa had a very close companion at FESAS known as Barry. Obinwa and Barry belonged to the same Anglican Church Choir at Aba,

Eastern Nigeria. Both of them sang special tunes together during Sunday services at FESAS. Maduora loved music. He found a link joining his dad, Obinwa and Barry, and that was choral music. He loved Obinwa and Barry too. The trio later adopted the name 'scientists' from the former Vice Principal of FESAS, Mr. Oluwaramipada. Barry later entered into University of Ilorin and studied medicine. Obinwa and Maduora entered into the University of Nigeria.

Obinwa was not officially assigned to room 325. He usually came to update his notebooks by 'scanning' Maduora's science notes. But as usual, one thing led to the other, the normal stories of jambites, he found a safe haven in room 325. He became the closest companion to Maduora because of his simplicity and truthfulness.

He continued with his athletic lifestyle and more Christian inclination. He was a fine gentleman and had very dark curly hair. His relationship with Maduora was symbiotic. Both of them respected each other.

He did not participate in most of the discussions in the room. Maduora expected so much from him during the discussions concerning the holiday exchange program.

Obinwa casually observed the passport photograph on the holiday exchange form; he endorsed the official holiday exchange plan. When the holiday came, Obinwa was not close. But it was understood by Maduora. If wishes were horses, beggars will ride.

EXIT THE DRAGON.

CHAPTER TWO

ENTER
THE TIGER

Whatever that means according to Bruce Lee. Egwuatu Aku is the tiger of the trium virate. True to his name, he fears nobody and he loves money. He does not fear his parents. I don't think he feared any deity at all. For the story context, once in a while, he appears in room 325 and disappears. Unlike the other owners and squatters committee members of room 325, Egwuatu was a second-year student of Philosophy, UNN. He comes to room 325 to remind Maduora that he and his roommates are 'ewu matriculas.'

Somehow, Egwuatu emerged as the Students Union Government Enjoyment Officer. Maduora mobilized his roommates during the SUG elections. And they massively voted to make sure Egwuatu defeated his opponents. Little wonder Maduora sometimes boasts that he is more highly connected than the rest of his roommates.

By the time Maduora got the opinion of his six roommates concerning the 'letter bomb', he was calmed down but he became more confused on the way forward. He later took the letter to Egwuatu's room at Eni Njoku Hall.

As the Enjoyment Officer of the SUG, Honorable Egwuatu converted his room into White House extension. The official UNN Students Union Government seat of power (White House) is Ladoke Akintola Hostel and Akpabio Hostel. The SUG president and other very important executive and cabinet members, reside mainly in rooms inside the White House. After winning the election and taking oath of office, Egwuatu refused to relocate from Eni Njoku Hall to Ladoke Akintola Hall or Akpabio Hall. Instead, he decorated and tastefully furnished his hostel room at Eni Njoku Hall and baptized it as White House extension.

Egwuatu was comfortably relaxing in his White House extension when Maduora brought the 'letter bomb' to him. Mere looking at Egwuatu's face while he was glancing at the passport photograph attached to the holiday exchange form, Maduora felt reassured that the shock the 'bomb' inflicted in his mind had disappeared. Like all the others who had read the letter, Egwuatu was excited. But he was calm same time. By the time he opened his mouth to speak to Maduora, Maduora was already awaiting his soothing words to calm his strained nerves. And so, having taking his time to masticate and digest the letter, Egwuatu merely chorused what Maduora's roommates had earlier said.

Typical of Speakers of House of Parliament, having gathered suggestions and debate points from all concerned, Egwuatu acted accordingly. It was like a c o n s e n s u s a g r e e m e n t a m o n g M a d u o r a ' s roommates, classmates and friends. Finally, and without mincing words, honorable Egwuatu said to Maduora, *"Lovett must come to Nigeria. Life."*

INTERLUDE ONE:

"Ikpe malu eziokwu, aka azu di ya.

SOME EARLY YEARS AT ORAGRAM.

Maduora Eze, Egwuatu Aku, Tagbo Ohanuzue and Dike Tylor lived in the same section A of H.A.G Offor House (dormitory) as class one students of Oracity Grammar School (ORAGRAM). Tobias Ene (aka Tarzan) was a class five student and lived in the same dormitory. In that particular academic year, the House Captain was Joe Nwokedi (aka khaki no be leather). Peter Chibeze (aka Akanna) was the Senior Prefect and Arinzechukwu Chianugo was the Chapel Prefect.

Other outstanding class five students of the same set are: Dan Obinaya, Geoffrey UdeGod, Edward Umeh (Buccaner), Chima Ubanna, Nnamdi Onyekwuluje, DBoy Umeh (Lemmy Kuti chitinous) and Edmund Ndukwe (Eddy kwangana – oho).

Tobias Ene has a very close resemblance of the ancient man. He also adopted the nickname 'Tarzan' without understanding the implications. His classmates call him Tarzan. The daring ones in his class like Chima Ubanna sometimes call him Tarzan Ozo (Tarzan the Gorilla). No junior student ever tried calling him Ta, not to talk of completing the Ta with zan or zanza. Any junior student who ever imagined calling him that name will literally be skinned alive.

One fateful morning, at about 6:45am, Maduora, Egwuatu and Tagbo were returning to their dormitory after the early morning preparation session. The trio was already dressed in their white shirts and khaki shorts school uniform. Suddenly, out of the blues, Tarzan jumped out of the dormitory on his way to the toilet. He saw the three innocent Class one students and then roared like a very hungry lion, "THREE OF YOU, KNEEL DOWN THERE!" In less than a split second and without thinking about from where the roar was coming, the three of them went down on their knees immediately. By the time they looked up, they saw Tobias Ene in front of Offor House tying a towel round his waist and getting ready for the bathroom. Other senior students saw the trio kneeling down and began to ask one another what offence these students committed. No one could ask Tarzan directly. When the House Captain stepped into the scene, other senior students thought that Tarzan will now set his captives free so that they can go for their breakfast.

All of a sudden, Tarzan quickly spit out the last drop of water he sipped while brushing his teeth. He turned angrily to the kneeling captives and roared again, "WHAT DID I HEAR YOU SAY?"

Grave silence fell in front of Offor House and the small flower garden. Who wants to dare Tarzan? I say nobody. But Tarzan heard a whisper. He quickly entered the dormitory, dropped his tooth brush, brought out his strong leather belt, jumped back to the small flower garden and got ready to pounce on his prey while other students were just watching. Gradually, Tagbo Ohanuzue raised up his little finger and told Tarzan he heard a whisper too.

Out of fright and hoping he would escape the envisaged greater punishment by saying the truth, Tagbo told the entire on-lookers that,

"Egwuatu si ka anyi kpoo ya Tarzan Ozo gbafelu oso." *(Egwuatu said we should call him Tarzan the gorilla and run away).*

There was uproar among the entire students. Even if the trio were innocent before their trial, they have now publicly munched the forbidden fruit plus the juice and meat pie (agbakpo). A junior student dared to call him Tarzan? To add salt to injury, Tagbo was flippant and his vocal cords voiced out ozo to Tarzan's face.

Sharply, Egwuatu denied whispering anything to Tagbo. Naturally, both of them said,

"Please ask Maduora to tell us what he heard."

Maduora responded by saying he heard nothing. The other students advised Tarzan to set Maduora free, and he did. Tarzan and the other senior students watched Egwuatu as he continued his denial and at the same time served the extra punishment prescribed by Tarzan. Tagbo served same punishment with Egwuatu but he wept bitterly for two reasons; Egwuatu, his fellow Class One student had misled him. Secondly, ikpe malu eziokwu (the truthful person became a convict).

[END OF INTERLUDE ONE]

CHAPTER THREE

THE MASTER PLAN

"... Every gambler knows, there's a secret to surviving, knowing what to throw away and knowing what to keep. Because every hand is a winner, and every hand is a loser, so that the best that you can hope for is to die in the street. .."

-*KENNY ROGERS*

Little did Maduora know that having passed the JAMB exam, he has endorsed gambling with his academic timetable. From the Oracity Grammar School he attended, he learnt that *"may your days be rough,"* was a kind word. He was yet to navigate through the rough days.

His brain swept into action, accepting responsibilities, admitting his faults, taking corrections and relying on his own judgment. He confronted his academic challenges as other first year students, trying not to re-sit any exam

At UNN, re-sit exams were code named, 'bye election'. Every serious student avoided bye election. Incidentally, medical students and Animal Husbandry students must pass all their courses each particular year. After re-sitting an exam and a student still fails one or more of his courses, other departments permit what is called 'carryover.' Faculty of Animal Husbandry does not permit carryover of courses. Maduora knew he had a tight rope to walk. Maduora put his academic needs on focus and then decided to gamble with the affairs of IASA.

When he finished speaking, no, no, not finished speaking like the gambler, I mean when he had spoken to his roommates, some of his classmates and friends, he turned back to his writing table. If you recall from the song, when the Gambler finished speaking;

"..., he turned back for the window, crushed out his cigarette,

And faded off to sleep,

But somewhere in the darkness..."

In contrast, Maduora was not a gambler (maybe he was a Jew man); he wrote two more letters and sent them abroad. One letter was addressed to Europe; the second one was addressed to the United States of America.

The official letter he wrote to Europe was addressed to the Information Officer of the IASA in the Netherlands. Maduora assured him that plans were already in motion to ensure the success of the holiday exchange visit of candidate Lovett to Nigeria.

The second letter was unofficial. It was Maduora's first letter to Lovett. It was addressed to Lovett Choice Jackson, Faculty of Animal Husbandry, University of Illinois, USA.

Maduora informed Lovett that he has many hands-on decks to make sure that her holiday exchange visit to Nigeria will be a grand success. According to the holiday exchange form which Lovett submitted to IASA, Kenya was her first country of interest. Nigeria was her second option. She changed her mind and made Nigeria her first option after she received Maduora's first letter to her.

Now that we got love, what are we gonna do with it?

No.., no.., no.., I don't mean the popular pop song. Please pardon me, I can't even remember the name of the artist that made the song popular. What I wanted to write was that Lovett felt she has gotten what she wanted from IASA, so what's she going to do next.

In less than ten days, Maduora got the reply of his first letter to Lovett. Trust Americans, the letter indicated that Lovett had paid for her trip to Nigeria. She enclosed a copy of her flight schedule from her travel agency. The travel agency document implied that Lovett will be in Lagos, Nigeria on Saturday, 18th July, 1987 using Lufthansa Airlines. The departure date from Nigeria after three weeks was also clearly spelt out on the travel document.

Maduora read and re-read Lovett's first letter to him. He beat his chest. He felt excited. He was happy. There was no atom of fear or tension. He realized that in his village, Irefi of Oracity, east of the River Niger, men are identified by their bravado.

Mbelede nyilu dike. Mbelede ka eji ama dike.

That means, unpredictability defeats the brave warrior. At the same time, the brave warrior will fight despite the suddenness of the attack. And like one of the polished, titled elder statesman of his community, Nze Frank Nzepuo put it, "The hour finds the man". Maduora convinced himself that he can cope with the unforeseen circumstances. He decided to move ahead.

Having considered the tight academic calendar confronting him and the chance of gambling with IASA holiday exchange program, Maduora was about to make a critical decision. He also dreamt about finding himself in God's own country after playing host to Lovett. He came to the conclusion that he might travel to America too. It was a good dream and a good idea.

At this point in time, Maduora never knew what a travel visa was. Dearly beloved, ladies and gentleman, viewers and listeners at home, readers and thinkers, browsing crew and internet scammers, my co debaters, a very responsive and smiling audience, accurate time keeper and you, the cheerful reader, this is the beginning of the American Visa story and not the job of many colors.

I hereby say welcome to the real story of the AMERICAN VISA honorable Egwuatu had, but Maduora never had.

The journey of a million miles begins with a first step, but some youths believe it's okay for Monkey to do work and baboon go de chop. One of the grand commanders of country music concluded one of his songs by saying;

"...Now please don't think I'm weak,
I didn't turn the other cheek,
And papa I should hope you understand, sometimes you got to fight,
When you're a man..."

"COWARD OF THE COUNTY"

– *KENNY ROGERS*

And so, Maduora sat down to plan his activities for the rest of the escapade.

CHAPTER FOUR

FURTHER
CONSULTATIONS

"Time will tell, time will tell,
Time alone, alone will tell.
When I was just a little boy, I was six years old.
I asked my daddy what he thinks my future holds.
He said son, you will grow up to be a man.
The facts of life, you will start to understand. . ."

-JIMMY CLIFF

Maduora had passed six years old, the facts of life; he was yet to understand, so he took Lovett's letter and all the related stuffs of jambitoes to his daddy at Enugu.

Voila Monsieur Mayaki, il et riche. Pourquoi? Parce qu'il a deux grand masons, et trois gros autos, Une femme, et dix enfants.

According to some funny old students of Oracity GrammarSchool, Osy Ojii, Osy Ocha, Mbaji Aniak, Ohayo and Zencity classmates,

"Le Francais n'agbam mgbo n'isi."

(Meaning: French Language scatters my brain like bullet).

I think I got this one correct. The English translation simply reads like this;

Look at Mr. Mayaki, he is rich, why?

Because he has two big houses, three big cars, One wife and ten children.

Thanks to Madame Elfreda Chizube Okoye (EC 4 Life) and Monsieur John Mbamalu, the French teachers I know.

However, Mr. Maduora Eze senior was a Pharmacist. He was a man of honor. He had one house. He also had about three cars at three different times. His wife passed on two years earlier. Monsieur Mayaki was richer than Maduora's dad in number of children but Maduora Eze senior was richer in the Holy Spirit.

He was a senior staff at the Ministry of Health Enugu. He worked and lived at Enugu, the state capital. Maduora senior was still overcoming the loss of his wife. He was excited seeing his firstborn son taking some bold steps towards being a man. After a pleasant tete- a-tete with his dad, what Maduora junior understood from his trip to Enugu was like the continuation of the lyrics of the song of Jimmy Cliff;

"...Nobody knows, just what tomorrow may be. So, I won't tell you now, but listen while I sing.
Dad will say;
Time will tell, time will tell, Time alone, alone will tell."

What Maduora did at Enugu was the presentation of his proposed action plan to his dad. Interestingly, Maduora junior was an old boy of Oracity Grammar School, Oracity, while Maduora senior was an old boy of the famous DMGS Onitsha.

Please o, DMGS does not only mean Does Monkey Go to School?

The correct meaning is, Dennis Memorial

Grammar School (Lux Fiat).

Despite the fact that both senior and junior Maduora Eze were old boys of grammar schools, Maduora senior completely understood what student holiday exchange meant, but Maduora junior did not.

Maduora junior got his dad's fatherly blessings and lots of moral support from his siblings. He returned to the university town later and the rest of the hosting plan went viral.

Before the receipt of Lovett's first letter to Maduora, there was no plan for the hosting of anybody during the holidays. All of a sudden, Maduora and Posha saw the flight schedule and travel details of Lovett. The rest of the holiday plan was the standard Nigerian fire brigade approach. I am sure you know fire rescue services doesn't work in Nigeria. But fire brigade approach makes Nigeria giant of Africa. If you recall preparations of our Super Eagles for football championships, you will understand what you are reading better.

"Two hearts, two hearts that beat as one. . ."

No…. No… No…, not the two hearts of 'Endless Love' by Lionel Richie and Dolly Parton. I know.

Do you mean Romeo and Juliet? Nope, just hold on.

As Maduora was hoping to get an American visa by hosting Lovett in Nigeria, Posha was hoping to get an American visa too by doing the same thing. Have you seen such two hearts? Oya;

Joggle ba, joggle ba, joggle ba n'egwu agbago

(Dance, dance, dance, music has come).

As the holidays drew nearer, Maduora found out that Posha travelled to Onitsha to arrange for funds and prepare accommodation for the august visitor in UNN. Posha also made telephone contacts with his relations in Lagos and got assurance that all is well. On his return to the university, Posha convinced Maduora that their plan to co-host Lovett was solid. Maduora was convinced Posha wanted a piece of the action. What Maduora was not sure of was the quantity of the action Posha will get. Definitely, Posha was not deterred, he continued the co-hosting holiday plans like there was no other alternative holiday plan. He committed his time and money and gave lots of words of encouragement to Maduora.

The arrival date for Lovett was 18th July. At UNN, the slang for the third terminal examination is 'almighty June'. This is because, unlike other tertiary institutions, UNN does not follow the semester calendar. They still run an academic session in three terms. During the third terminal exams held in the month of June, students are expected to answer questions that could arise from lectures concluded in the first term. So, the accumulation and expectation of exam questions from the first term to the third term made the older students refer to the third term exam as the almighty June. Some second-year students like Egwuatu took delight in frightening the jambitoes by reminding them of the almighty June exam.

Between April and July, Maduora stepped up the tempo of his holiday plans. He had earlier wanted to spend his holiday in Jos, North Central part of Nigeria. But Lovett's holiday plan had to supersede his own. Without compromising his attention towards his academic goals and with the fear of almighty June, Maduora vowed to himself, neither to let himself down nor disappoint his loving dad.

Series of meetings were held in room 325 Awolowo Hall, and in another room at Eni Njoku Hall. Due to the seriousness of each of the matters tabled, none of the meetings commenced if one out of the three conveners was absent. The trio had earlier agreed that as long as the agenda includes Lovett's holiday plan, the three boys must be physically present at each of the meetings.

From then on, Posha, Maduora and Egwuatu formed a formidable circumstantial and essential trio. The circumstance that necessitated the gang formation was the co-hosting of the American girl. The expected ultimate gain for the three teenage boys was to obtain the American visa.

Posha wanted his own American visa. Maduora dreamt of his own American visa. Subsequently, the minutes of most of their meetings sounds like one of the Nigeria's gentleman, Mike Ejeagha's song;

"Nnam eze akpata m enyi, nnam eze akpata m enyi,

 Nwa Mbe isi na ikpata onye (2x)

Asi m ani nya dube enyi, chebe enyi, Odika m si na akpata m enyi (2x), Okwa enyi ga abu isi oche (2x)?

Enyi na aga na m kwu gi n'azu (2x) Gwo gwo gwo, ngwo."

Well, not exactly the music, this is the inside of the story of the American visa Egwuatu desired and he got it. In Mike Ejeagha's folk tale music, the tortoise (Mbe) kept telling the elephant (Enyi), keep moving, I'm supporting you.

Meanwhile, the tortoise had concluded arrangements for marrying the king's daughter. The king accepted to hand over his daughter to the tortoise to be his wife if only Mr. Tortoise will present to the royal family a life elephant as bride price.

In analogy, Egwuatu kept telling Maduora that they are together but Egwuatu had really gone ahead of the trio.

Prior to their first meeting as members of a new gang, Posha and Egwuatu came from the same hometown of Ubasi, Eastern part of Nigeria. Both were strangers to each other in UNN. One of their first encounters was in Maduora's room 325. Posha claimed to be a former school mate of Hejike, Maduora's roommate. After several diurnal and nocturnal visits to room 325, Posha smuggled a mattress from God knows where into room 325. Posha secretly converted himself from a squatter to a member of room 325 Awolowo Hall.

A renowned business mogul tried that conversion method later after the famous June 12th election in Nigeria. After witnessing court proceedings at the Igbosere magistrate court on his return from self- imposed exile in 1994, K. O. A converted himself from a bloody civilian to the commander-in-chief of the Nigeria Armed Forces.

Posha succeeded, he later lived happily in room 325 but K. O. A did not enter Aso Rock. That's by the way sha.

Egwuatu also visits Maduora, his fellow community Grammar School friend in room 325. Egwuatu must have noticed Posha in this room 325 but never imagined that Posha could be anything else apart from the usual over one of the one thousand and one students of UNN. The fact that Posha had luxuriantly growing beards worsened Egwuatu's resentment of Posha.

One cool evening at Eni Njoku Hall, Maduora and Posha walked into a private room. It was identified as a private room because the occupant of the private room is a member of the Students Union Government, UNN. In short, Maduora brought Posha to the white house extension, the residence and office of the Enjoyment Officer, SUG, UNN.

After the traditional Igbo greetings and pleasantries, the first meeting of the trio together commenced. Posha and Egwuatu realized for the first time that they were from the same hometown, Ubasi. Egwuatu and Maduora attended the same secondary school in Oracity. While the meeting was going on, something strange happened.

Maduora started with the willingness he had to share the hosting plan of the American girl. He appreciated the interest and contributions made so far by Egwuatu and Posha. Posha continued by mentioning the positive steps he had taken so far towards the success of the co-hosting of the same American lady. Egwuatu, the tiger among the trio, saw a 'handwriting on the wall'.

The three adventurous boys spent about three intense hours deliberating on their chances and the odds against their mountainous escapade. Finally, having agreed to work individually and jointly towards the success of co-hosting the American Lovett. Egwuatu, Maduora and Poshality rose at about 11:55pm from the circumstantial first meeting of the trium virate.

CHAPTER FIVE

". . . Now I'm a lonely man trying to make life on
my own. Ever since the day I was born, I never
had a happy home.
Just like the river lapping, running
never cease. The day I was born in
the country, a little town. I'm
wondering now, just what my gain
will be. But it seems to me, happiness
I'll never see. Dad will say,

Time will tell, time will tell. . ."

In contrast to the sweet melody of Jimmy Cliff's evergreen hit track, Maduora relied heavily on his elite family background for material and financial support. He travelled out of the UNN to Aba, Abia State looking for financial assistance from one of his uncles.

His father's youngest brother was a highly placed judicial officer working for the Abia State Government. Maduora met his uncle named Chief Omife Eze inside his residence at Aba, the commercial city of Nigeria. Maduora quietly presented his case to Chief Omife. He needed moral and financial assistance to continue the co-hosting arrangement made so far.

Chief Omife was quick in his response. He never wanted to waste his or his nephew's time. He told Maduora bluntly, "I don't have enough money to cater for your frivolities."

Although Maduora attended a grammar school, he heard the word 'frivolities' first from Chief Omife that day. The next agenda was, does Maduora understand what frivolities meant? He was convinced his uncle is just and trustworthy, that is the reason he met Chief Omife first, leaving the other extended family relations. Maduora was discouraged for the first time concerning the holiday plans but he had no option than to obey his uncle.

It was certain Maduora was disappointed by the response he got from Chief Omife. He quickly decided to act immediately in order not to compound his pitiable financial predicament.

That same night, without consulting the two other members of his co-hosting crew, Maduora wrote his second letter to Lovett. He made sure he posted the letter the following morning. In the letter, he expressed his inability to go on with the hosting plan.

Maduora left his uncles residence at Aba the next morning and returned to UNN. He was obviously discouraged and disarmed but the reality is, Maduora doesn't even know what to do with Lovett if Chief Omife had given him the financial assurance he requested for. To him, it will be a big relief if Lovett cancels her holiday trip to Nigeria.

INTERLUDE TWO:

EASY ELSIE AND NWANMA NWAPA

Inside one of the compounds, along the street named Amechi Road, in Awkunanaw, Enugu, lived a very beautiful damsel named Elsie. While fetching water from the nearby local stream called Mmili ani, Elsie would pass in front of Maduora Eze family's residence. On her way returning from the stream also, she would pass through the same route. Sometimes, Maduora would notice that Elsie had gone to Mmili ani, he would do nothing else that day except calculating when Elsie would be returning from the stream. Maduora admired every step taken by Elsie. After watching midnight movies on NTA channel 8, Enugu, Maduora retires to his bedroom to dream about Elsie.

One bright Sunday afternoon, he mustered enormous emotional and spiritual courage. He invited Elsie to his daddy's house along the same street. Elsie dressed in a brown skirt, white blouse and a brown beret and walked into Maduora's sitting room. Elsie and Maduora had a very pleasant heart- to-heart chat that Sunday. Both of them were pleased with each other and they eventually fell in love.

While he was busy planning the holiday exchange program for Lovett with the gang, he never mentioned his escapade to Elsie. Elsie was then seeking admission into a higher institution of learning. During one of Maduora's visit to his dad at Enugu, he saw Elsie briefly. He tried to find out from Elsie which institutions she had written for admission. Elsie mentioned the names of about three different institutions located within the state capital. Maduora said to Elsie, "If you really want to acquire formal tertiary education, please seek admission from schools outside Enugu. There are too many social and commercial activities that will limit your academic pursuit. You can find good higher institutions of learning outside the state capital."

Maduora's love for Elsie was aflame when on his subsequent visit to Enugu, Elsie caressed and told him that she is now a first-year student of the Federal College of Education, Eha Amufu, Isi Uzo local Govt. Area, Enugu State.

Elsie became very friendly with two young teenagers while she was a first-year student of FCE, Eha Amufu. They are Chidinma and Mgbeke. Contrary to her name, Mgbeke was not timid at all. She was brought up in the vicinity of Alagomeji, Yaba, Lagos. She also left all the academic institutions in the former Federal Capital, Lagos to accomplish her quest for better higher education in a very remote village in the old Anambra State. It was Mgbeke's habit of being the first to make a comment among the trio that sometimes the two others call her Mgbeke the parrot.

Maduora rose up one morning, smiled to the rising sun.

Three little birds, (Elsie, Chidi and Mgby). Beside his door step, singing this song. The melody is pure and true, saying:

This is my message to you.

When Elsie expressed some doubt about her relationship with Maduora, the concluding part of the lyrics of Robert Nesta Marley's reggae hit is what Chidinma and Mgbeke sang to her. They musically reassured and told Elsie;

"Baby don't worry, about the things,
'Cos every little thing, gonna be alright."

The very first day Elsie introduced her heartthrob Maduora and his close friend Mr. Kene to her pals, Mgbeke nodded her head only. While in a gossip session and the usual blabbing of young ladies among their peers,

Mgbeke asked them, "Did you notice that Mr. Kene was speaking 'phoene'?" (Queens English that sounds as if it's coming out from the nose). While still dominating the gossip class, she forgot Mr. Kene's name and immediately described him as Mr. Clean Shave. The moment Elsie and Chidinma tried to figure out who Mgbeke was referring to, Mgbeke quickly said she was referring to Mr. Kenzy, Nwokeoma, Clean Shave, the difference is clear.

Due to the intense academic rigors and relatively poor social and economic scenario they encountered at FCE, Eha Amufu, Elsie (the Deaconess), Chidinma (the Prophetess) and Mgby (the Baptist), consciously and amicably changed their school address to Federal College of Education, Eha Afufu (the land of suffering).

Just like Maduora, Elsie was determined to overcome her academic challenges for two main reasons; she is the first child of her parents, and must neither disappoint them nor mislead her three younger siblings. Her second reason was to improve herself academically and sustain a healthy relationship with Maduora. Maduora always spared no available opportunity to assist her and always push up her academic cumulative average. Elsie and Maduora separately and mutually thought their love for each other will be consummated with Christian holy matrimony after graduation from their different institutions of higher learning.

Socially, Elsie, Chidinma and Mgby remained very good friends and sang almost all the hit songs of ABBA together. Three years later, they left FCE, Eha Amufu in flying colors. On their graduation eve, amidst wailing and shedding of tears of love, the trio sang the chorus of this popular ABBA track together:

"Knowing me, knowing you, aah.
There is nothing we can't do.
Knowing me, knowing you.
We just have to face it this time, we do. Breaking up is never easy, I know.
But I have to go.
Knowing me, knowing you. Is the best I can do."

Somehow in parallel, Maduora had lots of inhibited admiration for one of his uncle's sister-in-law named Nwanma Nwapa. Maduora's natural inhibition was that Nwanma is about eighteen months older than Maduora. Therefore, he never imagined attempting anything extra-curricular with Nwanma. Maduora's encounter with Nwanma was anchored in his Uncle Omeife Eze's residence in Aba, Abia State.

On one spectacular holiday visit inside Omeife Eze's residence, Maduora wanted to retire to sleep after watching the last midnight movie on NTA channel 6, Aba. Nwanma Nwapa also watched the movie but talked more than some of the movie actors. While the boring NTA movie was going on, Nwanma was busy describing and analyzing the steps and motives of each scene as if she attended that particular movie's audition.

Nwanma was very good in her use of the English language. She always selects and makes use of words that portrays her as a youthful responsible person. Maduora paid rapt attention to Nwanma's good choice of words in all life's circumstance. Before someone could shout Jack Robinson, Nwanma analyzed, dissected and re-enacted two bestselling movies for Maduora without watching NTA. The movie titles are **Celebrities** and **Blood & Orchids**.

The following morning, Maduora returned to UNN and tried sustaining the gist relationship with Nwanma by letter writing. If Maduora writes Nwanma with just one page of an official writing pad, in less than two weeks, he gets four pages of writing pad full of gist, humor, counselling and lots of encouragement from Nwanma.

If Maduora writes her with two writing pad pages, Nwanma replies him with four writing pads and four reverse pages with attachments for gist and words of wisdom. Somehow, Maduora told Nwanma about Elsie but somehow later, Nwanma knew more about Elsie than Maduora could imagine. While Maduora wrote separate letters to Nwanma in University of Lagos, and Elsie at Federal College of Education, Eha Amufu, Nwanma and Elsie wrote letters to each other. In her own colorful and separate letters addressed to FCE, Eha Amufu and UNN, Nwanma Nwapa motivationally counseled Elsie and Maduora respectively.

[END OF INTERLUDE TWO]

Immediately Maduora got to Nsukka Motor Park, he boarded a taxi and directed the taxi driver to move on to the White House extension. In the absence of Posha, Maduora told Egwuatu what he did at Aba. Egwuatu was disappointed with Maduora's statements and actions. But like an old tiger, he knew that

Maduora would fail in this escapade. After all, both were in the same class for five years at their secondary school. He knew exactly how Maduora will fail.

Egwuatu made it clear to Maduora that the planning and execution of the co-hosting agenda has gotten beyond the control of one man. He shouldn't have written that second letter and posted it without reference to the other two gang members. Egwuatu never felt discouraged. Truly, this was the right time for him to devour the two 'ewu matriculas' and escape with the 'bush meat' but his time was not ripe.

He subtly urged Maduora to write a third letter to Lovett. In fact, Egwuatu dictated, while Maduora wrote the letter. He made sure the words of the third letter countered all the issues mentioned in Maduora's second letter to Lovett. He humbly urged Lovett to disregard the entire contents of Maduora's second letter. Confidently, he stated that her hosting preparations have been concluded at UNN. All that was left was her presence.

While they were drafting the letter, Maduora disagreed with his dictator. His reason for disagreeing is that it will appear childish to Lovett if she gets counter letter from Nigeria.

He also mentioned that the second letter must definitely reach her before the third one gets to her. He seriously expressed fears concerning Lovett's security when she finally comes to Nigeria. To give more power to his fears, he told Egwuatu that the formidable trio they formed is incompetent and cannot cope with the security details required for their adventure. The above reasons given by the coward in Maduora only fueled the rage of the tiger in Egwuatu. Egwuatu did not shift.

Egwuatu assured Maduora that all is well. He suggested that Maduora should look for alternative sources of funds beyond his family. The Animal Husbandry Students Association (ASA) UNN chapter was mentioned as one of the organizations that could donate funds if properly communicated. Egwuatu for the first time mentioned that he can personally get some financial back up from the Students Union Government. Just before both of them dispersed, Egwuatu re-read the final draft of the letter, signed it and made a photocopy for himself. The third letter to Lovett was dispatched by DHL courier services.

During the immediate subsequent meeting of the gang held in room 325, Egwuatu did not waste time before telling Posha the blunder

Maduora had committed. To drive his point home and make it clearer to the two 'ewu matriculas', he presented to Posha the photostat copy of the counter letter he dictated and signed to correct Maduora's blunder.

This was the instance Posha's eyes were opened for him to see the 'hand writing on the wall'. Maduora saw the handwriting on the wall too, but there was no 'Daniel' in room 325 to give them the interpretation. Egwuatu has cleverly hijacked the co- hosting arrangements from the control of the trium virate. He quietly acknowledged the hidden submission of the two 'ewus' and decided, instead of devouring and consuming the goats immediately, he guided them steadily and remotely until Posha gave up and disappeared. And Maduora abandoned the holiday co-hosting plan of the gang. Egwuatu identified the gains of the co-hosting agenda. That is the American visa Posha wanted, Maduora dreamt of it, Egwuatu desired it. And like the tiger he is, he pounced on the prey and took a bite. But how?

CHAPTER SIX

". . . You've got to know when to go, know when
they hold on, know when they walk away, know
when they run. You never count your money when
you are sitting at the table. There'll be time enough
for counting, when the deal is done."

KENNY ROGERS.

Immediately after the 'almighty June' exams,
Maduora and Posha left UNN together for

Onitsha town. The initial understanding was that Posha will pick up some cash from a friend or a family friend and both of them will continue their trip to Lagos. Posha's initial arrangement for collection of the money failed.

Maduora had some cash from his dad. He also hoped to solve accommodation problems if any, by relying on his maternal uncle at Ebute Meta, Lagos. Posha tried to persuade Maduora that both of them can pass the night at Onitsha and proceed to Lagos the following day. Maduora felt one of them can proceed to Lagos that particular day while the other person can join the following morning. His reason is that it's better one or two people were absent during Lovett's arrival than the three of them not to be there.

At this juncture, nobody could predict Egwuatu's position. Egwuatu stayed back at UNN but he told the other two crew members they will meet at the Murtala Mohammed International Airport (MMIA), Lagos.

Maduora entered Lagos safely on Friday 17th July and proceeded to his maternal uncle's house at Ebute Meta. His journey from UNN via Onitsha and terminated in his uncle's residence took one whole day. His uncle lived near PAMCA International School at Ebute Meta. He intended to move from PAMCA to MMIA Ikeja the following day.

Before leaving Onitsha, Posha assured Maduora that both will meet before 7:00pm at the MMIA the same day Lovett is expected. Of course, according to their agreement before dispersing at UNN, Egwuatu will complement the gang at MMIA.

The crisscrossing happened at MMIA, Ikeja. On the D-Day, Maduora took off from PAMCA International School premises and stopped at MMIA. It was around 5:00pm, while walking around like a stranger in a new terrain, suddenly, Egwuatu appeared in the scene.

Egwuatu obviously figured out that Maduora has lost out in the co-hosting plans of the gang. Egwuatu started his own private agenda without easing out Maduora and Posha. He urged them on while executing his private plan. Check out Egwuatu's first step to edge out the other two gang members.

Maduora knew nothing about flight manifests. So, Egwuatu told Maduora that he has checked the manifest of the Lufthansa airlines and the name, Lovett Jackson is not in the list. Maduora did not understand what manifest was. So, he did not know there was need to double check the manifest. Back then, there was no mobile phone in Nigeria. Posha was inside the same airport, browsing the manifest.

Egwuatu and Maduora dispersed from MMIA but agreed to travel back to the east together through the local wing of the airport. Egwuatu purchased a flight return ticket from Enugu – Lagos – Enugu. That was why he appeared at the airport while Maduora was wondering where he could be. Egwuatu was aware Maduora had a one-way flight ticket, Lagos – Enugu. Both of them decided to meet again at the local wing of the airport without reference to Posha's whereabouts. When Maduora asked about Posha's position, Egwuatu showed no interest.

That same night, Lovett Jackson entered MMIA, Lagos, Nigeria. Posha saw her name in the flight manifest. The flight arrived on schedule. So many other things happened. The long-awaited holiday exchange program had started. The co-hosting trio and their guest from America were in three different parts of Lagos on 18th July.

At this interval, Maduora was yet to assimilate the real implication of the song Kenny Rogers sang above. All his actions were contrary to the beautiful pieces of advice The Gambler was preaching.

Maduora and Egwuatu left Lagos together on Sunday, 19th July on board Nigeria Airways first morning flight to Enugu. From Enugu airport, they joined a university professor in his official university car on the way to UNN. Shortly before boarding the flight at Ikeja airport, Maduora received some cash from Uncle Pamca. He counted it to confirm it was enough to take him back to UNN.

Somehow, Egwuatu was watching Maduora while he was counting the cash he received from his uncle. When Uncle Pamca disappeared from the vicinity and went back to Ebute Meta, Egwuatu walked closer to Maduora and said softly to his ears, "please give me some money, I will give it back to you". Maduora counted some fresh naira notes and handed them over to Egwuatu. A few minutes later, both of them entered the flight. Egwuatu knew the game very well, he played the gamble and got the money. Maduora never asked for a repayment of the money but the record of the transaction was never destroyed.

It was a very pleasant surprise to Maduora when he saw himself in room 325 before 12:00 noon on Sunday 19th July. He was excited also while telling his remaining roommates that he left Lagos this morning and now at UNN before noon. He tried to compare the short duration of the return flight against the long twelve hours he spent on the road while going to Lagos. He later calmed himself down thinking that after all, the tension Lovett Jackson's holiday plan triggered in him is now over. Egwuatu was deleted from his memory immediately both of them entered UNN.

Most of the other undergraduates have vacated the campus for the long holidays. Maduora started gathering the items he scattered during the almighty June exam. He packed his personal belongings and got ready to vacate room 325. It is noteworthy that Maduora met about just one or two persons out of the seven occupants of room 325 on his return from Lagos. The other four had completed their exams and vacated the campus.

When he was asked about the American lady he went to Lagos to receive, his response was simple, "She did not come."

The next morning, Maduora took his bucket, pillow and some note books to safeguard them in the lecturers' quarters. As he dropped the items, he decided to get in touch with his beloved dad's office at Enugu. He used the telephone in professor Emeka's house. Maduora felt free to use the telephone because professor Emeka's wife is a cousin to the senior Maduora Eze.

Maduora Eze junior had earlier discussed accommodating Lovett in professor Emeka's boys' quarters. Mrs Emeka was ready to ide the space from her boys' quarters. Unfortunately, Maduora did not get the space for Lovett because Mrs Emeka had assigned the room to a pregnant woman who needed the room during the Sandwich program.

While Maduora was talking with his dad on the phone, he learnt from his dad that Posha had earlier called Maduora senior's residential phone not less than three times. Posha wanted to find out Maduora's whereabouts. Posha left no doubt he telephoned from Lagos. His multiple phone calls put the entire Eze family in confusion.

M. Eze senior was aware his son had travelled to Lagos to receive his August visitor. But

Posha's phone calls from the same Lagos to him were a big concern for him. He masked his anxiety from the rest of the family over the weekend. So, when his office phone rang and he picked it up, hearing his son's innocent teenager's voice doused his tensed nerves. He only asked his son a few questions about the weekend trip to Lagos.

Maduora noticed that his dad heaved a huge sigh of relief when he picked his call. In his own answers to his dad's questions, he confirmed he was at the MMIA in Lagos two days earlier. He did not see the August visitor. He did not see her name in the manifest.

His dad calmly told him to make telephone contacts with Posha immediately. As far as he was concerned, Maduora junior just wasted his time and money, and also risked his life unnecessarily over the weekend. Luckily for Maduora junior, here is another opportunity to make amends before it becomes too late.

Maduora collected from his dad a telephone number and a house address at Isolo, Lagos. It was Posha's contact in Lagos. His dad offered him a flight ticket if he decides to get back to Lagos. Before concluding the telephone discussion with his dad, Maduora was already puzzled. He dropped the telephone receiver gently. He sat down on the sofa slowly. He stood up again. He did not know what next to do. He was worried. I think professor Emeka's daughter, Ada encouraged him to put himself together. His blood pressure was still very high when he eventually left the staff quarters and walked straight to Egwuatu's white house extension. Tension remained high because Egwuatu was nowhere in the white house vicinity.

Maduora waited patiently in one of the hostel rooms near the white house extension. About an hour later, honorable Egwuatu entered his room. He bamboozled Maduora by saying that he is just returning from an SUG cabinet meeting. Cabinet kor. Honorable Minister ni.

Maduora emotionally relayed to him the telephone discussion he just had with his dad. While they highlighted the skip on double checking of the manifest, both of them agreed that the best option left is for one of them to leave UNN immediately to go and assist Posha in Lagos. They hurriedly touched other related matters and then, out of anxiety, Maduora opted to bounce back to Lagos.

That very day, Egwuatu helped Maduora to

leave UNN and go to his dad's house at Enugu in the evening. Maduora bought a flight ticket from Nigeria Airways office at Continuing Education Center (CEC) building, UNN.

CHAPTER SEVEN

THE
LONE LONG
VACATION

The next morning, without having any other doubt in mind, Maduora boarded an airplane from Enugu to Lagos. His own lone long

holiday has been cancelled but Lovett Jackson's holiday exchange program has started. Lovett Jackson has left the United States of America and arrived Nigeria already. The anticipated chief host is in the air, puzzled. Egwuatu the tiger among the co- hosting trio is at UNN. Posha is in Lagos. But where in Lagos? Okay, assuming Lovett was at the same place with Posha in Lagos, does both of them know each other? All these questions were in Maduora's medulla oblongata at the same minute. No answer. Okay, just like a new generation Nigerian female artist, Omawunmi sang it, the truth is;

"If you ask me, na who I go ask?
The matter wey you see so, e heavy for mouth. No be
me go talk am . . . and so on.
If you ask me, na who I go ask?"

Maduora touched down at Ikeja airport, Lagos. Following the guidelines Posha gave to Maduora's dad on the phone, Maduora entered an airport taxi and moved straight to Idumota, Lagos Island. Inside the Idumota market, Maduora was looking for the person who can tell him where Posha is.

He got a reliable piece of information from Posha's contact person inside the market. From Idumota, Maduora entered another taxi that took him to Ire Akari estate, Isolo. The taxi route was Iyana Isolo.

Maduora took careful note of these areas not because he was planning to write a book. Rather, he was certain he was lost in Lagos. To him also, Lovett Jackson was lost. The person

Interpol or the Nigerian police will query about the missing American lady is Maduora. He tried to keep a mental record of his movements incase his dad eventually hears the news of his missing son. He hoped to return one day and tell his beloved dad the true story.

Fortunately, inside a fenced compound at Ire Akari estate, someone passionately told Maduora that Posha passed the previous night there. It was a comfortable house, maybe about two or three bedrooms and a parlor. It was neat. The compound was small but clean.

Maduora stayed in this house for some hours while waiting for Posha. His mind was not at rest. Maduora calmed himself down after long hours in Lagos traffic and a long-tensed search for his friend and august visitor. Somehow, Maduora learnt that Lovett came into Nigeria according to plan. Posha received her at the MMIA according to plan. The rest of the escapade was the manifestation of the beginning of the 'palace coup' planned, and is being executed by the tiger among the trio. The rest of the crew members were only pawns on the tiger's chess table.

Lovett and Posha had spent two nights in this modest house at Ire Akari estate. Lovett's luggage went missing on arrival in Lagos. She was asked to come back to the airport two days later. Incidentally, Lovett's luggage was recovered the same day Maduora bounced back to Lagos. Posha and Lovett returned together from the airport after retrieving the luggage late in the evening.

That same night, Posha arranged for the American and the two of them to spend the night in a hotel near Iddo Motor Park. The reason was made very clear to Maduora. Posha's friend who owns the house at Ire Akari estate travelled abroad and had immigration problems. Posha managed the situation maturely and to the admiration of Maduora.

In the hotel room, Posha asked Maduora what happened on the D-Day, Maduora managed and told him his own version of the story. Posha accepted the blabbing about not understanding what flight manifest meant. He saw Lovett's name in the manifest and that was why he waited and even called Maduora's dad with the airport's telephone.

Posha knew it was Egwuatu's game plan. At this juncture, the interpretation of the 'handwriting on the wall' flashed into Posha's memory. Egwuatu's inability to decode the contents of the flight manifest to the other two members of his gang at the MMIA was deliberate. Posha did not make this interpretation of the 'handwriting' known to the public too.

From then on, Posha decided to challenge Egwuatu by adopting the weird wrestling tactics of Amalinze.

– Remember Mazi Amalinze (aka the cat). The famous wrestling champion of **THINGS FALL APART**, by Professor Chinua Achebe. Amalinze reigned for several years as the village wrestling champion because his back never touches the ground. The challenger that defeated him and became the new Umuofia wrestling champion was Okonkwo. Somehow, fortune smiled away from Posha. His feet slipped in the escapade and Egwuatu became the 'Okonkwo' of this novel, '**AMERICAN VISA.**'

Majestically, Posha introduced Maduora to Lovett. They exchanged greetings and pleasantries. Maduora apologized for his absence at the airport for the reception. Having set a very conducive scenario for all three to interact, Maduora made the details of the hosting plan by the gang known to Lovett. She admitted that Posha was very kind and she is already enjoying Nigerian delicacies.

Early the next morning, the American lady, Posha and Maduora boarded a taxi at Iddo Motor Park. In the company of about three other passengers in a Peugeot 504 wagon, the holiday makers travelled eastwards towards the Niger Bridge of the River Niger.

The destination of the commercial vehicle was Onitsha, the popular commercial city, eastern part of the River Niger. It was a journey of about five hours on a good road. But due to the Nigerian peculiar poor road maintenance culture and police/armed robbers check points/road blocks, the journey lasted longer than expected.

The holidaying trio alighted from the public transport vehicle at Onitsha around 8:00pm. The two teenagers were convinced it was risky continuing the trip to UNN the same night. The two members of the gang conferred and smuggled themselves and their American guest into Ubasi town for safety.

Lovett still had some canned food for dinner. Maduora and Posha watched with amusement how she tried to mold eba without cutleries. She was completely relaxed throughout the duration of the tortuous journey to the east. Lovett was able to take a few snapshots with her camera in Lagos.

The following morning at Ugamuma village, Ubasi town, Lovett took more snapshots. Posha was not keen appearing in the pictures. Lovett was more interested in the landscape, native building designs, local fowls and other funny looking domestic animals in the village.

With the assistance of good friends and to the admiration of Maduora, Posha organized accommodation, breakfast and a private Peugeot 504 wagon car to convey the holidaying crew from Ubasi town to UNN. Despite the presence of a foreigner in his village, Posha had time in the morning to go and play football with his village teammates. Oh! My dear Posha;

Oya; Joggle ba, joggle ba,
Joggle ba n'egwu agba go.

The adventurous trio sneaked out of Ubasi town and made a brief stopover at Enugu. The request for the stopover was made by Maduora. Posha and the car owner/driver granted the request. The driver took the trio to Amechi road, Awkunanaw, Enugu.

Triumphantly, at his dad's residence, junior Maduora introduced Posha and Lovett to senior Maduora. Maduora Eze senior and his entire family felt very happy. Maduora Eze senior entertained his guests bountifully. All the guests and their host were filled with joy.

Photographs were also taken. The tension caused by the crisscross at the MMIA naturally disappeared. After about one quick hour at Enugu, the holidaying trio left Enugu for the University town, Nsukka.

Just before joining the express road leading to the ninth mile corner, Posha tried to make contacts with Okay High and intimate him on the progress of the holiday escapade. They could not make physical contact with Okay at Enugu. The 504 wagon drove slowly from Awkunanaw through Uwani, to Iva Valley and finally left Enugu.

The holidaying trio approached the ninth mile corner and turned northwards. As the vehicle advanced towards UNN, the beautiful hilly landscape, and the cool breeze from the quiet luxuriant grasslands of Nsukka engulfed Maduora, Posha and Lovett.

CHAPTER EIGHT

"Turning and turning in the widening gyre.
The falcon cannot hear the falconer. Things fall apart,
the center cannot hold. Mere anarchy is loosed upon
the world."
THE SECOND COMING – W.B. YEATS, 1919

The university town of Nsukka became a home
to the first Nigeria's indigenous Governor-
General, Chief, Rt. Honorable, Dr. Nnamdi
Azikiwe, the Owelle of Onitsha. Many

undergraduate at UNN then, felt very proud residing very close to the elder statesman. Zik of Africa chose a very conducive topography and located the great citadel of learning. Before then, he had travelled far and wide but chose not his village, Onitsha to reside. He lived most of his life after politics at Onuiyi Haven, Nsukka.

Maduora felt the holiday adventures of Lovett in Nigeria should begin with this scenario. He presented this point during one of the series of the meetings he had with the other members of the gang. First of all, - go down low, - the three members of the gang agreed that the first port of call for their august visitor was the vegetative grasslands of Nsukka and immediate hilly environs.

Within UNN, the crew and guests will likely visit the Faculty of Animal Husbandry, the UNN observatory, CEC, Arts Theater, etc. outside UNN and within the eastern Nigeria, Polo Field at Enugu, Ogbunike cave were listed. Yankari Game Reserve, Nigeria Wildlife Park, Jos, Northern Nigeria were all penciled down. But before moving out to visit these cultural and hospitality landmarks, the guest must pass the night somewhere.

Each time the issue of accommodation came

up during the famous gang meetings, there was never a clear decision. While the two others appeared less worried, Maduora always raised the question; "Which house are we going to keep our guest here in UNN?" Posha usually answered with a dry smile; "Don't worry yourself, everything will be sorted out."

If Maduora insists on an answer from Egwuatu, he merely chorused what Posha said, "don't worry, accommodation for Lovett is the least of our problems, just raise some money from anywhere." He confidently said to Posha and Maduora, "what you are looking for in Sokoto town, is right there inside your sokoto." Literally meaning, what you intend travelling to Sokoto town to find, is right inside the trouser (sokoto) you are wearing.

Maduora had thought he could just take Lovett to his dad's house at Enugu. But he had to work diligently and uphold the principles and codes guiding the adventurous members of the teenage gang. The gang could not secure accommodation from the UNN guest houses. While Posha and Maduora were travelling outside the campus looking for financial back up, Egwuatu stayed back in the campus attending SUG cabinet meetings especially enjoyment matters. And so, when the travelling duo entered UNN with their august visitor, their vehicle moved straight to the white house extension. Luckily, Honorable Egwuatu Aku, (OON), Enjoyment Officer, SUG, UNN, was standing by at the white house extension entrance.

Over ninety percent of the regular students of UNN have vacated the campus for the long holiday. It was the beginning of the end of one official academic year. A few regular students still hung around for one reason or the other. The campus was relatively quiet because some funny non-academic activities were still going on. Don't worry, the sandwich students started checking into the hostels as the regular students were checking out. In this scenario, the teenage trio officially welcomed Lovett Jackson back to Africa.

According to history, this is the under-developed home land of the great ancestors of the heroes of the black race.

Lovett told Maduora the following morning, "I had fun." Whatever that means, Maduora felt she was speaking through the nose. Her English grammar was typical American accent. Maduora discussed many issues with Lovett while they were in transit from Lagos – Onitsha – Ubasi – Enugu – UNN. He was more of a tour guide than anything else.

Lovett was cute, fair in complexion, tall and full of life. She appeared more admirable than her passport photograph. She also came from a responsible American family. She was fun loving and had a very good sense of humor.

Before the end of the first weekend, the crew had visited the Faculty of Animal Husbandry, the UNN Observatory, the UNN zoological garden, the Enugu zoo, Polo field and Amusement Park and returned to UNN. Well, there is a saying, "two is company, three is crowd." The gang members were not always together as Lovett was being guided in the holiday tour. Along the line, Posha disappeared from the scene.

Maduora travelled out of UNN and returned before the end of the second weekend.

He found out Egwuatu had forcefully opened his bag and taken something. He confronted Egwuatu. As usual, blabbing from Egwuatu to Maduora, meaning 'you can't do anything.' Maduora also noticed that Egwuatu had guided Lovett to the nearest bureau de change. Lovett had started spending her own money. Maduora knew he can't do anything about it. Lovett appeared to be okay with Egwuatu. In between the threesome of Maduora, Egwuatu and Lovett, the secret code is – 'See no evil, hear no evil, say no evil.'

With the apparent bravado which Egwuatu had demonstrated, Maduora felt assured that Lovett is safe in Nigeria. Maduora remembered what his fellow jambitoes of room 325 were saying before the arrival of Lovett. Now that Lovett is here, all the jambites disappeared like ewu matriculas.

Maduora admired the courage and strength of character displayed by Honorable Egwuatu. Maduora thought about so many other things. And lying lonely on his bed one night, he said goodbye to Lovett and the dream of his own American visa. Maduora was part of the holiday plans for Lovett. He stalled his original personal lone long vacation plan. But now, events with the gang has fallen apart.

CHAPTER NINE

UWA MGBEDE

In whatever you do in this world, your beginning is of less importance than your end. That's the moral behind one of the series of the folktale songs of gentleman Mike Ejeagha, the song goes like this;

". . . Uwa mgbede ka nma.
Oh Oh Oh, uwa mgbede ka nma."

And so, the story of the American visa Maduora never had is crowned with a happy ending. Whether you are an Arsenal,

Manchester United, Liverpool, Manchester City or Chelsea fan, you are likely going to join Maduora and Posha to joggle. If you are an Enyimba FC or Enugu Rangers FC fan, Abuja National stadium is now open. Just wait for the final minutes. of the extra time. Arsene Wenger is standing up already, Up the Gunners. The special one is smiling. Soon and very soon, we'll talk about FOOTBALL FRENZY and Femi and the gang of Nigeria info. 99.3FM – Please don't ask me how I cope with these guys. Just ride on. Our ordinary president, Dr. Ahmad Isah, and the world wide Brekete family, Human Rights Radio and Television, 101.1fm, una hembe lembe!

One morning in the last week of Lovett's visit to Nigeria, Egwuatu guided Lovett and Maduora from Ubasi town to a motor park in Onitsha. Egwuatu told Maduora to step outside the car. Maduora asked him why? Egwuatu calmly answered him, "I want to guide Lovett to Yankari Game Reserve and other cities in Northern Nigeria." Maduora knew Egwuatu did not need him for the tour. The motor park was not the place for him to make a request to be part of the tour. He simply stepped out of the car and as the driver moved on with Egwuatu and Lovett, Maduora bade them farewell.

Maduora went home sad, but his soul was happy. Sometimes when he remembers Lovett and Egwuatu, he feels confused. The truth is, Egwuatu lived his life the way he understood it. Maduora expected more understanding and show of Agape love from Egwuatu. Till this day, Maduora was always reassured that Egwuatu did not betray him. Maduora bore no grudges against Egwuatu.

The final note is, Maduora encountered a puzzle he could not resolve. His family and roommates were all excited and encouraged him but the noose on his neck in the middle of the adventure was cut by Honorable Egwuatu. Egwuatu set Maduora free but others felt Egwuatu displaced Maduora.

Two weeks later, Maduora returned to UNN to resume the new academic session. He got a letter from America. It was written by Lovett. She informed Maduora that she is safe at home in the United States. He sent some pictures and lots of words of appreciation. She promised that she will be of help whenever Maduora decides to visit the USA. Maduora was satisfied.

One week later, Honorable Egwuatu appeared in Maduora's new hostel, room 304, Alhaji Isa Kaita Hall. Both of them chanted and enjoyed the initial traditional Igbo pleasantries which usually come from one gallant warrior to the other. For example; while both of them were standing, Egwuatu and Maduora praised each other for the success of their adventure by hailing themselves with the following chants:

Egwuatu: Agu
Maduora: Agu n'ibe ya

Egwuatu: Dike ana akpa ogwu na anya, ona achi ochi
Maduora: Ofu onye ana ekene, unu abia go.

Egwuatu: Anu ana agba egbe, ona akpalu nni.
Maduora: Egbe belu, Ugo belu, nke si ibe ya ebena?

Egwuatu: Ga aga, ana ogwu.
Maduora: Ochu okuko nwe ada, nwa okuko nwe nwenwe oso.

Egwuatu: Anu kpolu nku na eju onu.

Maduora: Akpakana jide ozo, ozo ga ana.

The meaning of all these is that Maduora is a war lord in Igbo land. Maduora's responses also imply that Igbo land is blessed with a young warrior in the personality of Honorable Egwuatu.

He courteously entertained his friend the old

way reminiscent of their days at the Grammar School. While they were enjoying their goat meat pepper soup and bottles of soft drinks from the Isa Kaita Hostel canteen, Egwuatu slipped his hand into his cowboy mini jacket.

Making sure Maduora was in his best mood ever, Egwuatu brought out his International passport from his pocket. He flipped to the page where the visa was displayed and then he calmly said, "This is my visa to the United States of America." Maduora glanced through the document, congratulated Honorable Egwuatu and ordered more pepper soup and drinks for their merriment.

Lots of stories, rumors and gossips had spread throughout the campus about the escapade of the teenagers. But they drank and satisfied themselves and some other hostel members visiting the canteen. Just before everybody in the canteen dispersed, Maduora jokingly said to his friend, "you are hereby promoted from SUG Enjoyment officer to be the new Federal Minister for Enjoyment." The visiting crowd responded with a loud ovation and clapping of hands and spoons and bottles. One of their friends added, "A new Federal Minister for Women Welfare."

That night, alone in his new hostel room at Isa

Kaita Hall, Maduora tried to recollect his days as a first-year student in his former room at Awolowo Hall. In room

304 Isa Kiata Hall, the two students he met were studying Religion. Emeka Hill was in second year, just like Maduora. Big T. was in final year. He felt at home with these two, but really missed the crowd in his former room. He fell asleep after he remembered and mediated on the words of this song from;

Hymns, Ancient & Modern 257

1. Glorious things of thee are spoken.
Zion, city of our God;
He whose words cannot be broken.
Formed thee for His own abode.
On the Rock of ages founded.
What can shake thy sure repose?
With salvation's wall surrounded.
Thou may smile at all thy foes.

2. Savior, since of Zion's city.
I through grace a member am.
Let the world deride or pity.
I will glory in thy name.
Fading is the worlding's pleasure.
All his boasted pomp and show.
Solid joys and lasing treasure.
None but Zion's children know.

Twenty years later, Maduora traveled to Britain. Before the takeoff from the Nnamdi Azikiwe International Airport, Abuja, Maduora told Egwuatu, "you made your first trip to the America a long time ago, please handle me with care." Egwuatu asked him, "why? Are you not a man?" Maduora answered, "This is my first trip outside Nigeria, yours was 1987, exactly twenty years ago." Egwuatu smiled and said," interesting."

A few minutes later, both of them boarded a British Airways air plane. Just six hours later, they alighted at Heathrow airport, London. Maduora once more hailed Honorable Egwuatu and said,

"Nwoke na ibe ya ra, bu soso n'onu."

(All men are equal must have been publicized by a drunkard).

In order words, with what Egwuatu has achieved in the immediate past twenty years of their lives; Maduora could not believe that all men are equal. Maduora hailed Honorable Egwuatu severally, because Honorable Egwuatu is a great achiever. They both retired to sleep in Mr. Stan's apartment, along Shrub land Road, Daulston, Central London.

A few minutes after 5.00am, Maduora woke up

from deep sleep and smiled to himself. It was late October, one of the winter months in European countries. A scene in one of Eddy Murphy's popular movie, 'Coming to America' flashed into his medulla oblongata. He scratched his hair and scanty beards and quietly whispered to himself, tapra tapra tapra ta' as if he was discussing with two of his former classmates called Elder Statesman and Igwe Kaita.

He then sneaked quietly from the bedroom, passed through the sitting room and opened the small door leading into the balcony. He swiftly realized he was on the fourteenth floor of the twenty-two floors tower. He slowly touched the winter frozen rails and looked back. He saw a very dim reflection of himself in the sitting room glass window pane. He was excited by his own mirror image, the beautiful tall trees, the rooftops and street lights of London city. He cupped his palms round his mouth, looking directly over the rooftop of the neighboring shorter buildings, and seeing some early morning risers walking down the shrub land road, Maduora screamed,

"Good morning my neighbors." He repeated the greeting two times in English language and once in vernacular (ututu oma o, umunnem), looking alternately to his left- and right-hand side.

He did not expect anybody to respond because he knew he was not In Igbo land where such greetings are excitedly and mutually acknowledged. He was just remembering a movie he watched while he was a first-year student of UNN far back. He looked at the improvised mirror again and saw something that looked like Santa Claus (Father Christmas). He momentarily stuck out his tongue and gently caressed his sprouting moustache with his right and left fingers simultaneously. He put the tip of his thumbs on the tip of his two ears. He spread the rest of his fingers and turned to the pedestrian street light, tall slender trees, squirrels and pigeons.

He screamed again, "Good morning my neighbors" The pigeons stopped singing and one of them responded with a surprised soprano voice, "Praise the lord." The squirrels stopped jumping and one with a fluffy ear shouted with slow baritone voice, "Alleluia somebody." Maduora opened the sitting room door quickly, looked back only once and said,

"Halleluaiah, Amen," and then ran inside the room.

When Egwuatu woke up from slumber thirty minutes later, he asked Maduora, "I heard your voice and some other voices a few minutes ago, please what were you doing outside?" Maduora answered, "I greeted my neighbors." Egwuatu smiled and probed him further. "Please, which one are you, Eddy Murphy or Arsenio Hall?" Maduora replied, "Eddy Marsenio Hall." Egwuatu called out their sleeping host, Mr. Stan.

Mr. Stan confirmed that he also overheard Maduora and some other funny voices early in the morning. Egwuatu quietly and softly told Stan that this is Maduora's first trip outside Nigeria. Maduora quickly signaled Egwuatu and said to him in vernacular, "wenite onu (louder please)." The pigeons that gathered outside flew into the air and scattered in different directions. The squirrels increased their paces and jumped unto trees farther away.

INTERLUDE THREE.

Years back in ORAGRAM, Maduora, Egwuatu and Tabgo joined the Igbo cultural Society and became foundation members of the Oragram cultural dance troupe. They learnt to study, work and dance together. During the annual inter-house sports competition hosted by the school principal, Sir Isaac C. Udokanma, the trio of Maduora, Egwuatu and Tagbo represented Offor House in the cultural (atilogwu) dance group. While still in class one, they learnt the Offor House anthem;

Thy moving song, Offor house (4x).
I know. I know, I know thy moving song (2x).
Move on Offor, move on Offor.
This is thy moving day. Move on little pilgrims,
While the streams are flowing
Move on, Offor move on.

During the practice session for the cultural dance, the Class One students freely relax with their seniors respectfully. The greatest comedian of the Class One set was Christopher Modebe. He learnt to dance very well and added acrobatics and lots of swagger to his dance steps. The atilogwu dance group was led by Andrew Ocheta and David Ejikeme (secretary, and the long gong beater). Christopher Modebe (aka Ozo di mgba) was always able to hear and interpret the sounds of the Alo (long gong). In one of the initial comedy scenes he created, he demonstrated the sounds of the gong to the full admiration of all members of the dance group. While David Ejikeme was beating the gong, the dancers moved their waists and mba ji (lower leg muscle) in tune and rhythm. Christopher translated the sounds of the gong and flutes like this;

John brown - Ogboji (2x).
Nya na nne ya - Ogboji.
Nya ya nna ya - Ogboji.
Fa tulu ji n' Ose - Ogboji.

Several years later, when Maduora joined Egwuatu in UNN, Egwuatu and Maduora reminiscences their atilogwu dance years. Inside the Awolowo Hall or Eni Njoku Hall canteen, they talked about their renown flutist, Louis Obiekwe (aka YoYo). Mbu uzo egwu (first line dancers) lyke Onukwube, Mikel Akabakee, Daniel Otenkwu, Chuma Nzepuo, Chikezie Anagbaso and Peter Obi.

While Egwuatu advanced to third year, Maduora also advanced to second year in UNN. After the celebration of their individual and collective accomplishments (passing JAMB, passing the almighty June and co-hosting of Lovett), Maduora and Egwuatu would share goat meat or fish pepper soup and toast with soft drinks from the hostel canteens. On Egwuatu's prompts Maduora gladly demonstrates the evergreen John brown-Ogboji dance steps.

ARIVAL FROM UNITED KINGDOM.

A couple of years after his return from London, Maduora discovered some of the old letters he received from Elsie and Nwanma Nwapa. It was fun to him re-reading love letters written over twenty years ago. When Maduora met Nwanma in her husband's residence at Lekki, Lagos, he told her that he has some of those letters she wrote to him while they were teenagers.

Nwanma could not believe her ears. She told Maduora, "if you really have one such letters, please give me. I will like to re-read it quietly to myself." Maduora smiled and replied her, "Of course I have the letter from the archives. In addition to that, I have the one where Elsie's name was mentioned several times." He calmly continued, "It will be handed over to you now, but please, call your teenage daughter to come and read it first, and to the hearing of both of us."

Nwanma flew out of her seat in excitement. When she paused her laughter to speak again, she continued laughing and waited for Maduora to pause his own laughter. Nwanma took a deep breath and looked Maduora straight to his face, and then said softly but firmly, "Capital No." And she asked, "How can my teenage daughter read the letter I wrote to a teenager of the opposite sex, when I was a teenager?" she insisted and repeated herself in vernacular, "Mba nu (capital) NO."

Maduora obediently surrendered the letter to his marriage counselor and just relaxed. After confirming the date and authenticity of the letter, Nwanma quietly read the letter and made a renewed comment. Having gone through one of the counseling letters she wrote herself, she concluded and told Madura, "Frankly speaking, Elsie is the best wife Maduora never had."

Somehow, somewhere else, Elsie met Maduora shortly after the funeral service of Pa Maduora Eze. Maduora senior had joined the Saints Triumphant at the ripe age of eighty-five. Elsie was admired by Maduora's siblings who gathered together to bid their great icon the final farewell. One of Maduora's younger sisters told Elsie, "If my brother had married you, he would have been a very accomplished man just like our great icon."

Elsie had completed her National Youth Service Corps (NYSC) program and got admission to pursue a degree course at the Enugu State University. She happily got married to a multi-talented barrister, Nnamdi

Nnorom. Both of them have four children.

Maduora got married about two years after Elsie and was blessed with four children. When Elsie mentioned the comment by Maduora's sister, Maduora smiled and looked at Elsie like they were teenagers once again.

One moment Elsie was expecting something more important from him, Maduora held her right palm briefly and left her again. He then smiled to her and said, "When my sister said to you that my family would be happier if I married you. She was right, except that she was not referring to you." Elsie was puzzled but still held on for him to land properly.

He took one funny step further away from Elsie and continued talking to her alone.

"My sister was referring to a cousin of ours. Her name is Elsie. And she is very fond of me. She is known within the family as Easy Elsie."

Elsie laughed heartily as she used to do in her teenage years. She knew that as far as Maduora was concerned, there was no other Elsie. Far back then, Maduora used to call her Easy Elsie.

Both of them talked about Mrs. Nwanma Nwapa and the counseling they received from her. Elsie also recalled that it was Maduora that introduced her to the Full Gospel Business Men's Fellowship International (FGBFI). Elsie had sustained her membership for several years. As they were parting once again, they held their hands together and sang the FGBFI chorus together;

His banner over us is love. (2x).
He brought us into his banqueting house.
And his banner over us is love.

END OF INTERLUDE THREE

A couple of years later, Maduora called the GSM telephone number of Poshality. Momentarily, Posha did not know who called him because he did not have Maduora's GSM number in his contact list. As of old, when Posha dropped his handset, he laughed heartily because he was happy.

He remembered the cheers from his fans, back in the days at UNN. He remembered his swings and fanciful swagger in the defense department of the First Year Medical Students Association (FYMSA) football team. He remembered how Stephen Keshi won the African Cup of Nations as Player in 1994, and as a Coach in 2013. He remembered Arsene Wenger of Arsenal. He remembered the jogging from Sir Francis Akanu Ibiam Stadium to the cluster of ripe mangoes between NSLT and the Carver Building at UNN. He remembered the mini mango party in room 325 Awolwo Hall back then.

Posha sat down and tried to restrain himself from the hilarious explosion in his head. The voice that sent him down memory lane was familiar. He could not resist the urge any longer and Maduora knew exactly what was going to happen. - You better join Posha dancing. Immediately Posha picked the call, Maduora started chanting to Posha's enjoyment;

Oya, joggle ba, joggle ba,
Joggle ba n' egwu agbago

CHAPTER TEN

JESUS CHRIST is neither a man like fictitious names we just read in this book, nor a human being like men and women you know. Jesus Christ is God. The bible teaches us about God the Father, God the son and God the Holy Spirit. Three personalities in one. The three members may differ in manifestation or appearance. All the three members of the trinity are essentially the same. Jesus Christ is the express image of God the father. He is the visible image of the invisible God. He is the physical and tangible manifestation of the God head. In Jesus Christ God came into the World in a form that he could be seen, heard, observed and emulated. God came into the World as a man named Jesus, for the purpose of redeeming lost mankind.

I was personally convinced about this trinity in January 2015. By July of the same year, my first novel, **POULTRY EVENTS,** the amazing story of a Macho King was published in Lagos, Nigeria. A few months later, my second novel, the **AMERICAN VISA**; the escapade of Lovett and the gang was completed. My message to the youth Worldwide is taken from the red-letter words of the King James Version bible, Mark 11; 23 & 24.

For verily I say unto you, that whosoever shall say unto this mountain, be thou removed, and be thou cast into the sea; and shall not doubt in his heart, but shall believe that those things shall come to pass; he shall have whatever he said.

Therefore, I say unto you, what things so ever you desire, when you pray believe you shall receive them and you shall have them.

The manuscripts of my first two novels were written in 1995. With my renewed belief and trust in God, my books became successful books in the Nigerian publishing industry 2015. Just keep your hope alive. Let's not forget the powerful slogan of the first African American President of the United States of America, Barack Obama, - YES, WE CAN. Surely, we can do all things through Jesus Christ that strengthens us.

As we journey through the stormy sea of life, let's not live a life without prophecy. Let's examine two major characters in the bible to help us understand why Maduora was able to enjoy his life within and outside the UNN despite the fact that he did not get the proverbial American visa.

The first character for browsing here is Jacob. When Jacobs's mother was pregnant, Rebecca went to ask God according to Genesis 25; 22b. In verse 23, the Lord gave Rebecca a prophecy. The Lord also told her that Jacob shall be served by his elder brother.

If Jacob was aware that his elder brother Esau will serve him, he wouldn't have bought the birthright with his own plate of porridge or nkwobi. If Jacob was aware, he would be a great Nation, he wouldn't have suffered and served his father -in-law for fourteen bitter years. All he needed to do was to live a normal life, and then God who created him, you and me, will work out His (God's) plan.

The second character for browsing is Jacob's eleventh son, Joseph the dreamer. When Joseph was seventeen years old, he had dreams which meant that he will be greater than his elder brothers. He did not struggle like his dad Jacob. His elder brothers sold him off and wacked the money.

But twenty-two years later, just by interpreting fellow prison inmates dreams and Pharoah's dream, Joseph became a Prime Minister. You can read his complete biography from the Genesis book of the bible. The way to discover your own success and distinction pathway is by connecting to your creator by your dreams and words of prophecy.

Every life has a purpose. Every human is created to have dominion over all the earth. (Genesis 1; 26-28). Revelation precedes manifestation. The light of revelation is required to fulfill purpose and manifest destinies. Until you know who you are, you will not start being that person. Until you know what you can do, you cannot start doing it. Until you know what belongs to you, you will not start enjoying it.

True success and prosperity is a function of revelation, not western education.

Education at the highest stage is the education of the spirit man. It gives man access to the deep things of God, which are beyond the scope of man's natural capabilities. When a man's mind is developed with education and information, the spirit should also be developed with revelation. Man can only truly know God by revelation, neither by education nor westernization.

I know you enjoyed reading the story of Lovett and the gang, but I want you to know what God told Joshua in Joshua 1; 8.

*This book of the law shall not depart out of your mouth; but you shall meditate therein day and night that ye observe to do according to all that is written therein; for then you shall make your way prosperous, and you shall have **GOOD SUCCESS**.*

Many graduates found out that what made them successful in life are not basically their academic qualifications. Names are too numerous to mention in this context. So, in this internet age you can easily Google these names and you will discover they achieved good success just by applying the code of Joshua 1:8.

Please Goggle names like: Bishop Mike Okonkwo of TREM, Bishop David Oyedepo of WINNERS, Pastor W.F. Kumuyi of DEEPER LIFE. Pastor David Ogbueli of DOMINION CITY. Pastor E. A. Adeboye of REDEEMED. Gbile Akanni of Peace House, Gboko.

These men have University degrees and something extra.

Please let's not forget, David was a young lad without formal military training when he killed General Goliath. By the time he concluded his forty years reign as the second King of Israel, he was popular in songs and dancing. He never missed an opportunity to thank God who made him what he is (Psalm78; 70 -72). Let's check a little of King's David songs in Psalm 36;7 & 8.

How excellent is your loving kindness, oh God!
Therefore, the children of men put their trust, Under the
shadow of your wings.
They shall be abundantly satisfied, With the fatness of
your house; And thou shall make them drink,
Of the river of your pleasures

This song is still being revised and chanted as classical music in Anglican churches worldwide. Lets' see how King David, the lion of the tribe of Judah assured us that God never fails Psalm 37; 25.

Since I was young, but now am old;
Yet, I have not seen the righteous forsaken,
Nor his children begging bread.

It is vital you and I should sing along with King David and the saints triumphant, by preparing the rest of Humanity, for Eternity, with Divinity.

Please with your permission, may I conclude this book and drop my feather pen with these words of prophecy that guided my footsteps from the days of my Youth till today. My life is a success story. I can as well chorus the beautiful song my dad, Ebenezer taught me on his eightieth birthday;

My life has been a joy to me,
No matter where I go.
I've learnt to live in harmony, With kindly friend of foe.

And so, back through the years, I go wondering once again, back to the seasons of my youth. I recall... no no no not again.

Okay, for the last time. I recall... these words of prophecy that helped me start my veterinary practice; skills and family life. Luckily too, it came to me as a song far back in 1996.

Please let's browse just one of prophet Isaiah's prophecies. I understand and enjoy it from the Igbo version of the Bible, Isaiah 41; 10.

Atula egwu, gi ka m nonyelu.
Elela anya gburu gburu n'ujo.
N'ihi na Mu Onwem bu Chineke gi.
Na agba gi ume.
Mu, ga enyelu gi aka. Mu, ga eme kwa gi nma.
M' ga eji aka nri nke ezi omume m, kwalite gi.

Fear Not, for I am with you, be not dismayed,
For I am your God. I will strengthen you,
<u>Yes, I will HELP you.</u>
I will uphold you, with my righteous right hand.
(NKJV).

One more irresistible melody please, as we finally step out of the jungle with the gang.

Psalm 40; 2 & 3

Onaputa wom n'ala apiti.
Omewo ka m guzo n'elu oke nkume. Otinye wo abu uto n'olu m ta.
Abu otito, Alleluia.

He has delivered me from the slippery sand.
He has set my feet upon the great rock.
He filled my mouth with sweet songs today.

A SONG OF PRAISE, ALLELUIA!

GLOSSARY

1. **Ewu Matricula:** First-year students of tertiary institutions.
2. **Jambites:** First-year students of tertiary institutions.
3. **Mbe:** Tortoise.
4. **Ozo di mgba:** Gorilla.
5. **Mba ji:** Gastrocnemius muscles, vertically under, and behind the knee.
6. **Agbakpo:** Meat pie or hard bread loaf of Oracity Grammar School.
7. **Kor. Ni:** Whatever
8. **Phoene:** English language with swag.
9. **Uwa Mgbede:** Tales by moon light
10. **NTA:** Nigeria Television Authority
11. **Ose:** Yam market at Onitsha
12. **Ogboji:** Yam conference committee.
13. **Egwuatu:** Fearless
14. **Maduora:** Selfless man; man of the people

QUESTIONS

1.   Posha was the leader of the gang. If yes, discuss. If no, discuss.

2.   Maduora Eze senior had certain similarities and differences with Monsiuer Mayyaki, please mention them.

3.   On the arrival date of Miss Lovett from the USA, the three gang members were at different ocations, please mention the location of each of them.

4.   Maduora and Lovett became university graduates some years after the escapade. Please what did they study in the university?

5.   Maduora and Egwuatu were good friends, both of them travelled to America together, true or false?

6.   At UNN, the room provided for the august visitor was baptized to what?

7.   Maduora and all male characters in this story were academically Science inclined. The

writer demonstrated his love for Art In some ways. Can you please identify them?

8.   If you enjoyed the story, please can you suggest two alternative titles suitable for a story like this one?

9.   Do you know you can write your own story and make lots of money? If yes, what is the title of your own first story book?

10.   Have you identified your calling? Have you read the manufacturer's manual for life on earth? The bible is the manual for sustenance of life in planet earth. Read and meditate on it daily. As you read the bible on your own privately, you will discover the secret for preparing humanity, for eternity, with divinity

JOB OF MANY COLOURS
By Amaefuna C. Udechukwu (AU. 2015)

1. Back through the years, I go wondering once again. Back to the seasons of my youth.
I recall the choice of jobs someone gave us.
And how my daddy put the choice to use.
There were dogs of many colors, every fowl was small. And I didn't have a job, it was way down in my teens. Daddy showed the choice(s) together, showing every dog with love.
He showed my job of many colors, that I was so proud of.

As he showed he told the story, from the Vet that he had met.
About the job of many colors, Jacob did then he said.
I hope this job will bring you, good luck and happiness. And I just couldn't wait to do it; daddy blessed me
with a kiss.

My job of many colors that my daddy made for me. Made only for rats, but I did it so proudly. I know we had no money, but I was rich as I could be. Doing my job of many colors, my daddy made for me

2. So with drugs in my syringes, holes in both my shoes.
Doing my job of many colors, I hurried off to work. There to find the others laughing, and making fun of me,
In my job many colors, my daddy made for me.

Though I didn't understand it, for I felt I was rich.
I told them all the love my daddy showed in every choice.
I told them all the story, daddy told me while he showed,
And how my job of many colors, was worth more than all their jobs.

They didn't understand it, as I tried to make them see. One is only poor, only if he chose to be.
Although we had money, but I was rich as I could be. Doing my job of many colors, my daddy made for me.